Boxed In!

a Dr. Gideon Box/Donovan Creed Novel

John Locke

TELEMACHUS PRESS

This book is a work of fiction. Names, characters, places and incidents are either the product of the author's imagination or are used fictitiously. Any resemblance to actual persons, living or dead, or to actual events or locales is entirely coincidental.

BOXED IN!

The publisher does not have any control over and does not assume any responsibility for author or third-party websites or their content.

Cover Designed by: Telemachus Press, LLC
Copyright © Shutterstock/136944005

Visit the author's website:
http://www.donovancreed.com

Published by: Telemachus Press, LLC
http://www.telemachuspress.com

ISBN 978-1-942899-79-2 (eBook)
ISBN 978-1-942899-80-8 (paperback)

Version 2016.01.10

10 9 8 7 6 5 4 3 2 1

Medical Warning

Talk to your doctor before beginning a John Locke series, as studies have shown them to be habit-forming and highly addictive. Do not read Locke if you suffer from high blood pressure or other heart-related issues, as readers often experience mood swings, increased pulses, elevated heart rates, and have reported unexpected shifts in body position that take them to the edge of their seats. Do not drive or use machinery while reading Locke novels.

Locke novels are not for everyone, and may cause serious reactions including insomnia, night terrors, and uncontrollable, maniacal laughter. Tell your doctor right away if you have these, or if you experience unusual changes in your behavior including heightened sexual urges, palpitations, or prolonged erections. Common side effects include confusion, hysteria, and trouble swallowing a given premise.

Do not drink alcohol while reading Locke novels, though those with a history of drug or alcohol abuse may be more prone to understanding the material. Adverse reactions to Locke novels include nausea and vomiting, loss of appetite, severe itching, rectal bleeding, purple spots under the skin, and Jimmy Legs. In extreme cases, readers have reported laughing so hard they not only shit their pants, but other's pants, as well. Upon completing a Locke series be prepared to experience symptoms of withdrawal, including fear, anger, extreme sadness, and moderate to severe depression.

Ask your doctor today if John Locke novels are right for you!

Personal Message from John Locke:

I love writing books! But what I love even more is hearing from readers. If you enjoyed this or any of my other books it would mean the world to me if you'd click the link below so you can be on my notification list. That way you can receive updates, contests, prizes, and savings of up to 67% on eBooks immediately after publication!

Just access this link: http://www.DonovanCreed.com, and I'll personally thank you for trying my books.

Also, if you get a chance, I hope you'll check out Dani's website:

http://www.DaniRipper.wordpress.com

John Locke

New York Times Best Selling Author

8th Member of the Kindle Million Sales Club

(Members include James Patterson, George R.R. Martin, and Lee Child)

John Locke had 4 of the top 10 eBooks on Amazon/Kindle at the same time, including #1 and #2!

...Had 6 of the top 20 books at the same time!

...Had 8 books in the top 43 at the same time!

...Has written 30 books in five years in six separate genres, All best-sellers!

...Has been published throughout the world in numerous languages by the world's most prestigious publishing houses!

...Winner, Second Act Magazine's Story of the Year!

...Named by Time Magazine as one of the "Stars of the DIY-Publishing Era"

Wall Street Journal: "John Locke (is) transforming the 'book' business"

John Locke

New York Times Best Selling Author
#1 Best Selling Author on Amazon Kindle

Donovan Creed Series:

Lethal People
Lethal Experiment
Saving Rachel
Now & Then
Wish List
A Girl Like You
Vegas Moon
The Love You Crave
Maybe
Callie's Last Dance
Because We Can!
This Means War!
Boxed In!

Emmett Love Series:

Follow the Stone
Don't Poke the Bear
Emmett & Gentry
Goodbye, Enorma
Rag Soup

Dani Ripper Series:

Call Me!
Promise You Won't Tell?
Teacher, Teacher
Don't Tell Presley!
Abbey Rayne

Dr. Gideon Box Series:

Bad Doctor
Box
Outside the Box
Boxed In!

Other:

Kill Jill
Casting Call

Kindle Worlds:

A Kiss for Luck (Kindle Only)

Non-Fiction:

How I sold 1 Million eBooks in 5 Months!

Dedication:

For: Nick Cate

...And for Jackie Fish, who famously said:
"If you take me to Inspiration Point I'll give you
A memory to last a lifetime."

Boxed In!

Introduction

A few years ago the Institute of Medicine issued a report that said physicians accidentally kill patients on a scale consistent with the holocaust.

Prologue

I

"SO THIS GUY *walks into a bar and...*"

I hate entering bars without a date because I always feel like "this guy" from the jokes. You know the guy I'm talking about? The one who walks into the bar with perfectly good intentions, but winds up getting pissed on, shit on, bear-fucked, or locked in a barrel giving blowjobs to bikers?

Word to the wise: if you ever walk into a bar and see *anything* unusual, but *especially* a midget in a cowboy hat, a talking dog, or a camel humping an alligator...you need to turn your ass around post haste.

Unless you're dyslexic: because who wouldn't want to be the dyslexic guy who walks into a bra?

That said, here I am, walking into a tavern, alone, taking a seat at the bar. But this time—*within seconds!*—a young, astonishingly pretty woman takes the seat beside me, flashes what can only be described as a *very* friendly look, and says, "If I told you my name was Jackie Fish, would you believe me?"

I look her over. "Do you happen to have a pet alligator, camel, or talking dog?"

She gives me a strange look, as if she might bolt, so I quickly add, "Yeah. I believe you're Jackie Fish."

She smiles. "Cool. Who're you?"

"Gideon Box."

"Seriously? That's crazy!"

"I agree it's an unusual name, but I wouldn't consider it *crazy*."

"I just meant it was a coincidence."

"How so?"

"I used to date a guy named Gideon," she says. "A golfer."

"Really?"

"Well, 'date' might not be the right word. It was more like a secret fucking arrangement."

I've heard it said the average American has a working vocabulary of about 5,000 words, and I'm sure every woman within a thousand miles knows the words *secret*, *fucking*, and *arrangement*. But those who look like Jackie tend not to put them together in the same sentence. Since she did, there's only one thing to do: I motion the bartender to pour her a drink. He does, then says, "Five dollars," and Jackie looks at me to see if I'm in the game.

I nod, hand him the five, then snap a shiny quarter on the counter and push it toward him.

"For you," I say.

He stares at the coin like it's something he's heard described by others, but never personally witnessed. Could it be some sort of shiny alien turd, and radioactive?"

"It's a quarter," Jackie says, helpfully.

The bartender sets his jaw and regards me the way elite publishers regard a John Locke manuscript: with horror, confusion, and rage. He leaves the quarter untouched, shows me his middle finger, and stomps to the opposite end of the bar.

It's not that I'm cheap, I just want private time with Jackie. And if there's one thing I've learned about bar pickups it's this: if you try to woo a cute young thing at the counter, the bartender will constantly hover nearby, to listen in on your game. By insulting him with a two-bit tip I've effectively guaranteed we won't see him again. The downside is if I want to get her drunk we'll have to go somewhere else. But isn't getting her somewhere else the whole point of a pickup?

Jackie seems to think so, since the next words out of her mouth are: "Is that your Porsche outside?"

"How'd you guess?"

"I saw you drive up in it, and you don't seem like the sort of guy who'd steal a car."

"Thanks."

"But then you tipped the bartender a quarter, so..."

I laugh. "I was just fucking with him."

She gives me a skeptical look, but takes a healthy sip of her drink.

I wait till she sets her glass back on the counter before saying, "Tell me about this guy you were secretly fucking. Was he a professional golfer?"

She laughs. "Not even. He was the club pro at a small golf course. We were having an affair. He was my best friend's husband, and like I said, his name was Gideon. He used to have this theory that trees are 90% air. You believe that?"

"Do *you?*"

"I have reason to. Wanna hear why?"

"Of course. I love a good story."

She fiddles with her napkin a bit, then says, "Three months ago I was fucking Gideon under a giant tree beneath a cliff near Waynesville. He was on top, really giving it to me, when—all of a sudden—his head exploded."

"Uh...I'm a doctor, so...."

"Dude! I'm not exaggerating! His head literally *exploded!* He *died!* I fucked a guy and his head exploded and he *died!*" She stares at me as if trying to discern something from my expression. Then adds, "Is there nothing you want to *ask* me about this experience?"

"Did you cum?"

She does a double-take. "Are you *kidding* me right now?"

"I don't mean *after* his head exploded. I was just wondering if you got off before he died."

She looks at me like it's 2007, and I'm representing South Carolina in the *Miss Teen USA Pageant* ("*And such as...*") Then she says, "You don't have many friends, do you?"

"Not so many."

She nods. "It's okay. You're twice my age and weirder than shit, but—and this might surprise you—I've been with worse."

"Thanks."

She takes another sip. "To answer your question, no, I didn't cum. But the whole head-exploding thing gave me a mental block."

"In what way?"

"I haven't had an orgasm ever since."

"Wow. Three whole months, huh?"

She pinches one of her nipples through her blouse, and pulls on it, making me wonder if I could use this subliminal "tell" to my advantage were she and I to play strip poker someday. She catches me looking, but doesn't call me on it. "You promise that's your Porsche out front?"

I pull the keys from my pocket and dangle them so she can see the logo.

"I won't lie," she says. "That means a lot."

"Why?"

"It's on my bucket list. I always wanted to ride in one."

She watches me finish my drink. Then says, "Know what else is on my bucket list?"

"Tell me."

"Getting fucked in a Porsche."

I try to maintain my cool, saying, "I thought you had orgasm issues."

"I do," she says, tilting her head to focus on my eyes. "But say we're fucking in your Porsche later tonight. Will you really give a shit if I fail to achieve orgasm?"

"I like your attitude. Just to be clear: are you offering me sex in return for a ride in my Porsche?"

"What're you, a cop?"

"Nope."

"What *are* you?"

"A welder."

"Really? Because a minute ago you said you were a doctor." She takes one of my hands in hers; turns it over, checks my palm. "No wonder you have no friends: you're a lying sack of shit."

I take out my wallet, show her my driver's license.

"So we're back to being a doctor?"

"Surgeon."

She looks confused.

"I didn't think you believed me when I said I was a doctor."

She gives me a long look, causing me to ask: "Have I killed the moment, or is your offer still on the table?"

"Are you asking if I'm still willing to fuck you for a ride in your Porsche?"

"That's what I'm asking."

"Would you consider tossing in two hundred dollars?"

"Are you asking me for two hundred?"

"Yes."

"You're worth ten times that."

"I agree. But I'm not a hooker, just a girl trying to get away from a very bad man. I had to leave rather suddenly, and—"

I hold up my hand. "No need to explain." I peel four fifties from my thick roll of cash. Then, because her eyes are bugging out, I peel off four more.

She looks at the money and says, "Are you sure?"

"Like I said, you're worth far more. But I *will* insist you grant me one concession when we have sex."

"What's that?"

"You're on top."

She laughs, takes the money, says, "Fine. But give me a good ride, 'cause if my head explodes I wanna go out with a smile on my face."

"I'll do my best."

"I'd expect no less from a doctor."

"Surgeon."

"Right." She takes my hand in hers again and says, "Just so you know, not many welders drive Porsches."

"Good point."

She says, "Not to brag, but I'm probably the best lay you'll ever have."

"I like your confidence. Tell me more."

"I'll make you cum so hard you'll set off car alarms from here to Pittsburgh."

"I hate Pittsburgh."

"No problem. For an extra hundred, I'll throw in Pittsburgh."

I smile, and hand her an extra hundred, 'cause we both know what this is all about. I'm not offended she's a hooker. In my experience she's worth two grand, and here I am, getting her for $500.

She lifts my hand to her lips and kisses it. Then says, "Is your name really Gideon Box?"

"It is."

"That is such a totally cool name! By the way, you're under arrest."

"I beg your pardon?"

"Solicitation of prostitution. I'm a cop."

II

SHE'S A COP?

Shit!

Now what? Should I make a run for it, or trust my high-priced attorney to make a case for entrapment? I instinctively turn my head to look for the nearest exit, but Jackie says, "Eyes on me, Dr. Box!"

I turn to face her.

She says, "Put your hands where I can see them."

I sigh, hold up my wrists.

She gives me a look that's not quite pity, not quite empathy. "Are you really that desperate, or just the sad, gullible loser you appear to be?"

"You mean gullible because I thought I could pick up such a pretty girl so easily?"

"No. I mean gullible because you think I'm a cop."

"You're *not*?" I lower my hands, place them on the counter. "You're not a cop?"

"Of course not. Are you *insane*?"

"Almost certainly. But about the cop thing: that wasn't cool. You really—"

"Gideon?"

"Yeah?"

"If you take me to Inspiration Point I'll give you a memory to last a lifetime."

"What do you mean?"

"Think about it."

I do. Then say, "Sadly, I have no idea where that is. But how about we just—"

She puts her hand over my mouth and says, "You've got five seconds to say yes."

I don't need five seconds: "Yes!"

Chapter 1

FOUR HOURS EARLIER...

IF YOU HAD to pick a staff member to represent our hospital in a beauty contest—and I urge you not to—you could do a lot worse than Nurse Jennifer.

A *lot* worse!

Which is not the same as saying she's drop-dead gorgeous.

She's not.

But she's a solid 9, so when you suddenly encounter this level of beauty among our raggedy hospital staff you can hardly believe your good fortune. The odds are roughly equivalent to winning the lottery, discovering the mother who abandoned you as an infant in Bangladesh, or finding an honest reporter at *The New York Times.*

It's late afternoon, I'm halfway through my board-mandated rotation, and the ER is already swollen to capacity with the dregs of humanity. Scanning the lobby I see a dozen familiar faces: patients I treated for other serious injuries as recently as two days ago, which validates the Law of Inverse Value which states: the less you contribute to society, the more trauma your body can withstand.

While heading to an exam room to consult with a new patient I get distracted by the happy sight of Nurse Jennifer bending over the water fountain at the far side of the waiting room. I make a snap decision: the patient can wait.

Expertly navigating my way through the wretched throng, I ignore the needy, the seedy, the drug-addled, crazed, and forlorn patients who reach out to me like the zombie cast from *The Walking Dead*. As I steadily advance through this sea of despair, something deep within Jennifer's DNA triggers her fight or flight mechanism, causing her to suddenly bolt for the *Staff Only* door. Unfortunately for her, she fumbled her key card long enough for me to shout, "*Jennifer!* Hold up!"

She freezes as she must, for I'm a doctor, and technically her superior. She turns, takes a deep breath, and waits as I deftly sidestep the guy who's attempting to remove a non-existent bullet from his arm with a box cutter, and the transvestite in the poodle-skirt who's dry-humping the homeless guy. The homeless guy spots me and shouts, "I've been waitin' six fuckin' hours!"

"Waiting's good," I holler back. "It means your injury's not critical."

Now, standing before Nurse Jennifer, I say: "Gotta love the ER, right? The people are to die for, and the work? Wow! So rewarding!"

She rolls her eyes.

I wanted to catch Jennifer alone, because you wouldn't believe how easy it is for a doctor with my pedigree to get into a young nurse's pants, especially one like Jennifer, who's been on the job less than two weeks.

"Thanks for waiting," I say. "I needed to tell you something."

"What now?" she says, with great annoyance.

"I wanted to apologize for raising my voice to you earlier. It was rude of me."

"I agree," she says, icily. "Except that you didn't raise your voice, you yelled at me in front of the entire team."

"I...well, I suppose I did. I'm very sorry."

"Apology accepted. Now move along, doctor. We both know I don't like you."

"I don't blame you for that. But I *do* want it on record you were right and I was wrong." (Of course I was wrong: I purposely yelled at her for no other reason than to set up this phony apology so I could win her over after the fact. I learned long ago, quite by accident, that it softens women up when a guy who appears to be a jackass turns out to be humble).

She says, "You *were* wrong. But I'm surprised to hear you admit it."

"It's the right thing to do. Fact is, I was upset about something else and took it out on you." I pause a moment, trying to decide if I should mention my sister's gruesome death in Chicago Thursday night, during a horrific home invasion. That would probably create empathy and stir up all sorts of other beneficial emotions in Jennifer, but it also might cause her to wonder what sort of person would want to go out on a romantic date less than a week after hearing the news about his sister. Not to mention the almost certain buzz kill our relationship would suffer if she talks to the other nurses and learns I've never had a sister.

I decide to use my New Start strategy: I smile and say, "I really like you. Can we start over?"

She laughs. "There's no 'we,' doctor! Correct me if I'm wrong, but my understanding is you don't even *work* here! You're being punished, forced to perform community service, or whatever. You'll be gone in two days."

"Maybe so, but I *do* happen to work at this very hospital."

"Yeah. On what the nurses call Millionaire's Row."

"Don't hate me for *that*! Not when it could work to your benefit."

She shakes her head. "Wow. *There's* a line if I ever heard one."

"I'm serious, Jennifer. I think you might have what it takes to be a member of my practice."

"You mean boobs?"

I feign a hurt look. "Are you not aware I've been interviewing young, capable nurses to join my surgical team?"

"No. I'm only aware you're trying to blow smoke up my ass."

"How could you possibly think that?"

She laughs. "Gosh, that's a tough one! Maybe it's because I doubt my two years at community college qualifies me to assist the world's foremost pediatric heart surgeon."

I refrain from mentioning my other credentials. Not because I'm modest, but because I want her to *think* I am. After she agrees to a date she'll look me up online and see all my accomplishments. When she brings it up at dinner I can pretend it's no big deal. In the meantime, it won't hurt to give her false hope about moving up the career ladder, so I smile and say: "You may not be fully qualified yet, but with the right training, who knows?"

Her expression says she's not buying a word of it, but her mouth says, "Why me?"

"We're a perfect match: your interest is neonatal nursing, and my practice is devoted to saving the lives of infants who are considered hopeless cases."

"There are dozens of fully-qualified neonatal nurses between your suite and my basement."

"Maybe so, but they're dinosaurs and battleaxes: good at what they do, but opinionated as hell, and hopelessly set in their ways."

"They're excellent caregivers," she says.

"True, but they're a generation behind."

"In what?"

"Treatment protocol."

"How so?"

"My patients are hopeless case children and infants. Every doctor, specialist, and surgeon they've seen has given up on them. As far as the hospital's concerned, these kids are dead before they enter my OR. So when I finally *do* get them, I already know standard treatment protocol didn't work. If it *had*, they wouldn't have sent them to me. So I operate—dare I say it?—*Outside the Box.*"

She groans at the expression, so I move right into the pitch: "Why do I think you'd be a great candidate for my practice? You're young, bright, empathetic, and eager to learn."

"Like all new nurses."

"Yeah, but today I got the opportunity to see your dedication. I'm not kidding, Jennifer, I *saw* something in you today. I *noticed* you."

"I noticed you too, doctor."

I smile. "Thank you."

She says, "I couldn't help but notice the way you felt the need to publicly humiliate me."

My smile fades. See? This is the problem with good-looking nurses. No one ever yells at them. It's no secret I treat my current staff of ass-faced nurses like shit and make their lives a living hell, but they deal with it because we're saving lives. That said, I *do* have constant problems with my older nurses. If I tell one of them to flip a baby over so I can try something that occurred to me on the fly, I don't have time to hear warnings about why I shouldn't. I need a nurse who'll flip the kid immediately, without asking questions, and who won't report me to the Board afterward. I *know* they're not supposed to flip a kid over or upside down when I'm holding its heart in my hand, just as I know I'm not supposed to cuss these infants, slap them around, or whisper in their little ears that I'm going to murder their parents if they die on my watch. But I do all that and worse because my job is to do whatever I have to do to save their lives. And before you rush to judge me, consider this: I've saved 72 out of 72, which means there are 72 children in the world who would have been dead if I'd followed standard treatment protocol.

Jennifer almost certainly knows I've never lost a patient, and that should count for something. She probably also knows I lose nurses all the time. And yes, of *course* there are dozens of highly-qualified neonatal nurses in our hospital. They used to work for *me*! I feel like telling Jennifer to get over herself and shut the fuck up about our altercation. But the fact she hasn't slapped me yet tells me I'm still in the game. "You impressed me, Jennifer. I know how hard your job is, and believe me—"

"*Do* you, doctor?" she interrupts. "I doubt you have the *slightest* idea what I have to deal with. I'm the newbie, which means I get the jobs the other nurses—and even the orderlies—refuse to do. On top of that, I have to deal with assholes like you!"

"That seems like a harsh thing to—"

"I nearly lost my *job* today because of you!"

"*Seriously? Over that?*"

Now I know how General Patton felt when they told him he couldn't slap his soldiers. I take a deep breath, let it out slowly, wondering why I'm willing to work so hard to get what will probably amount to B-grade pussy. Then I show my sincere smile and say, "You have every right to be pissed at me. But I absolutely *do* understand how hard your job is."

"Tell me."

"Nurses do 90% of the work, get none of the credit, and all the blame. You put in longer hours than me, and do so without losing your temper or abusing your authority. I wish I could be more like you. I *want* to be more like you."

"You're patronizing me."

"I'm not. Who can possibly doubt that nursing is one of the most physically and emotionally demanding jobs in the world?"

"Every doctor I've met."

"Not me, Jennifer."

She gives me a look. "Just to be clear, which type of nursing are you referring to, Dr. Box? Medical, or breast-feeding?"

I ignore her sarcasm and say: "During the course of an eight-hour shift, nurses lift 1.8 tons of weight."

That gets her interest. "You pulled that number out of your ass!"

"I did not. It's a fact, easily verified. Nurses are on their feet constantly, moving heavy equipment, lifting patients in and out of wheel chairs and hospital beds. 3,800 pounds a day, and that's just the physical component. Hospitals are notoriously understaffed, which means you're overwhelmed with more patients than you could possibly care for. Still, your ass is on the line when things go wrong."

"That's certainly true."

"Your stress is off the charts. You deal with human tragedy, trauma, loss of life, and have to interact with frightened, angry, grieving family members looking for reassurance, and someone to blame. You can't help but get emotionally vested in your patients. When you lose them, it leaves a hole in your heart."

She looks at me through new eyes.

I lower my voice, move in for the kill: "Jennifer, I've been miserable since the moment I yelled at you today, and

I'd give anything if you'd let me make it up to you. Is there any possible way you'd consider having dinner with me tonight?"

"No. But I *will* accept your apology and politely ask you to fuck off."

What?

Stunned into silence, I finally stammer, "Are you sure?"

"Do I *sound* sure?"

She does.

—Okay, so maybe Nurse Jennifer wasn't the best example. But trust me, I get my share of young nurse pussy. And patient pussy, too.

And the ugly, grateful *wives* of patients.

Like Gail Garner, who you're about to meet....

Chapter 2

GAIL GARNER'S A Satan Superfecta: addicted, ugly, rich, and menopausal. Came barreling into the emergency room like she owned the place, demanding we move her husband, Harold, to the front of the line.

I don't know this bitch, but she's got enough clout that the triage nurse upgraded Harold's condition to serious, put him in an examination room, and paged me to meet him at my earliest opportunity. I happen to know Harold entered the ER complaining of a backache, so I took my sweet time answering the page. Had my conversation with Jennifer at the water fountain, and now, walking back through the waiting room with my tail between my legs, pause to watch an appallingly drunk teenager vomiting a bucketful of puke into his lap. My first instinct is to pass quickly, before the scent hits my nose, but I can't help but notice the kid's mom, and wonder if I'm about to witness something truly special in this random moment of human suffering. Specifically, I'm moved by the way his mother gently props him up before racing to the restroom for paper towels. I can tell she's furious with him for being publicly intoxicated, but she's his mom, and loves him, and is clearly worried for his safety. I wonder if the little shit has any idea how lucky he is, and immediately get my answer: as she rushes back from the restroom and begins working diligently to clean the mess from his pants he tilts his head back, looks at her through half-closed eyes, and says, "Suck me, gorgeous!"

I don't care who you are, what you do, or whatever you see wherever you work: Emergency Room duty has you beat.

I enter Harold's exam room to find Gail shaking, and scratching her neck and arms as if suffering from an allergic reaction. I introduce myself and ask about her recent fornication experiences. She how-dares me, and slaps my face, which I consider an odd response, since she's the right age, and fornication's a common side effect of hormone withdrawal, whose symptoms include crawling, itching skin sensations.

I banish her from the room and turn my attention to Harold, who, like 90% of the people who enter the ER, is *not* experiencing an emergency situation. Even worse, he's faking his symptoms. Don't get me wrong, he's making all the right moves, saying enough of the right things to prove he's a back-pain veteran, but tonight?

Not even close.

Over the next 30 minutes it becomes clear that Gail's using Harold's fake condition to score pain pills to feed her own addiction. Now, after giving Harold one last look of disgust, I open the door and motion one of the nurses to send Gail over for a consult. As she approaches, I say, "We'll want to keep your husband for three days and nights."

She blanches. "*What?*"

I gesture in Harold's direction. "I gave him the strongest medicine possible, but that pained expression has never abated. It's clinging to his face like shit stains in a wino's underwear."

"His face *always* looks like that."

"Maybe it's because he's truly in pain."

She glares at Harold a moment, then shouts, "Are you *kidding* me? I don't have time for this! Just write him a scrip for Vike and some muscle relaxers, and I'll take him home."

"Vike?"

I *was*, in fact, kidding about keeping Harold, knowing it would set her off. But Gail should know better than to ask for a specific brand of pain killer. Since *all* narcotics bind to opioid receptors, patients who ask for specific brands are usually re-selling, if not personally abusing the drug.

She says, "Check his records, doctor. This isn't his first rodeo. Trust me: a week's worth of Vicodin, he'll be fine."

There it is again: Vicodin.

I'd love to tell you I'm such an accomplished student of the human condition I can spot a pill popper from a mile away, but I only learned about Gail's addiction after Harold spilled his guts while under the narcotic I gave him. He told me plenty, but the fun fact I learned is he's never allowed Gail to see him *full-frontal*, as they say in Hollywood. This, because his mother—a mean drunk—routinely violated his private area with cigarettes during his formative years.

Sad story, right?

Again, not true.

I know, because while Harold was unconscious I treated myself to a peek at his twig and berries and guess what I found out about his private area?

Chapter 3

HAROLD'S CROTCH IS perfectly normal: standard-issue penis, properly-formed testicles, no sign of burn marks or abuse of any kind. He's deliberately deceiving Gail. But why? Could it be he's suffering from some sort of mental condition?

My educated guess is: who gives a shit?

What sort of bastard—twisted or otherwise—would lie about his mother abusing him? Normally I'd give him a dose of PID (physician-induced diarrhea) for making such a slanderous accusation, but my dislike of Gail trumps my disgust for Harold, so I decide to fuck with her, instead. To that end I lower my voice and say, "Mrs. Garner?"

"Yes?"

"We need to talk."

She gives me a nervous look, but says nothing. I motion her to follow me to an empty corridor, where I ask, "How much do you know about Harold's condition?"

"Everything I need to know. He sneezed and threw his back out. Case closed. End of story."

I show her a practiced look of concern. "I'm not talking about his back. I'm referring to his...uh...private area."

She purses her lips, furrows her brow. "What does that have to do with his back pain?"

"In order to give him a proper diagnosis, I had to lower his pants. When I did..."

She gasps. "Are you accusing me of *abuse?* Because that wasn't me! His mother burned him with cigarettes when he was a child. It was quite traumatic."

"There's no evidence of abuse, Mrs. Garner."

"What do you mean?"

"Have you never seen him naked?"

"That's none of your business."

"Quite right. I only thought you should know what I found. I apologize. I'll keep it to myself. Sorry to have bothered you."

She stares at me a moment. Then says, "When can we leave?"

"If you're dead set on taking him home tonight, we can start the discharge process immediately."

"Thank you. And the Vicodin?"

"Here," I say, placing eight individually-wrapped pain patches in her hand.

She glares at them with such contempt you'd think I deposited 4 ounces of warm sperm in her palm when she wasn't looking.

"What the fuck is *this?*" she seethes through clenched teeth.

"Place one on Harold's back near the source of his pain every three days. If he experiences any adverse effects—which you'll find described on the back of each wrapper—discontinue use and call his primary care physician."

Gail stares at me through contemptuous eyes and does that kind of slow boil you used to see in cartoons, where the character morphs into a thermometer and the red flows up from her feet and explodes out the top of her head.

"Relax," I say, giving her my magic wink.

She cocks her head with sudden interest, because that magic wink elevates my status beyond anything you'd believe. I may not have Bradley Cooper's looks, or the late Steve McQueen's charisma, but there's an entire segment of the female population that finds me irresistible, and yes, I'm talking about addicts. Admittedly, most of these women are as bitchy and ugly as Gail Garner, but even the nice-looking ones would push Cooper and McQueen aside to have sex with me, if it means getting a steady supply of their drug of choice.

I remove a pillbox from my pocket and watch Gail's eyes track it like a predator tracks prey. I open it, show her the Vike, and witness her instant transformation from Satan's dominatrix to a woman you could almost consider fuckable.

Almost.

Her features soften. She smiles seductively, opens her mouth and flicks her tongue against her top lip to demonstrate she'd blow me right here and now for what's in the pillbox. I'd let her, too, since I can think of nothing more satisfying than bringing this bitch to her knees after all the shit she gave our nurses earlier. But two things are preventing me: one, the intercom is crackling with activity that will soon include my name, and two, I've already got sexual plans for later tonight with a woman who hates me above all the earth's creatures.

Gail's holding the pain patches, I'm holding the Vike. "Want to trade?" I ask.

She nods.

I say, "Just to be clear, Harold's discharge papers will show I gave him eight pain patches to use as directed. Understood?"

She nods.

We make the exchange, I start to walk away.

"Doctor?"

"Yes?"

"Can I have your cell number? You know, in case Harold might need more...*pain patches* later in the week? I promise you won't be disappointed."

"How can you possibly make that promise?"

"Because I'd do anything—*anything!*—to ease Harold's pain."

"In that case..."

I give her my number. Not because I'm desperate for shame sex, but because "anything—*anything!*"—covers a lot of ground.

"I'll text you my number," she says.

"Thanks. Maybe I'll call *you* first."

She smiles. "Sorry I slapped you earlier."

"No problem. I get that a lot."

It's true. She's not even the first woman who slapped me *today!*

Gail moves closer, lowers her voice. "What were you going to tell me?"

"About what?"

"Harold's private area."

I look into her eyes. "Surely you're aware Harold's a woman."

"*What?*"

"Female of the species?"

"*Huh?*"

"He has an oyster. A taco. A bearded clam. He's Camp Oprah. Not Three Stooges."

"That's...*absurd!*"

"I agree. Stooges rule!"

"No. I mean...all jokes aside, what are you saying, exactly?"

"Are you familiar with the cult film *Harold and Maude?*"

She stares at me blankly.

"If they ever do a remake, and Harold auditions for a starring role, he'll play Maude."

She shakes her head. "How can you possibly *say* that?"

"When I lowered Harold's pants, a prosthetic penis disengaged."

She does a double-take. "You're having sport with me."

"Not at all! The good news is, you live in New York, so your marriage is valid. The bad news is, your husband's your wife."

She cocks her head. "I notice you're not saying his penis was surgically removed."

"That's correct. He's all bun, no meat. In Harold's case, hips *do* lie."

She stares at me incredulously. "You're absolutely certain?"

"When the penis disengaged, Harold rolled onto his back and tried to re-attach it, but I noticed a vertical smile where a stub should be."

"What about his testicles?"

"Surprisingly life-like. In a dark room I probably wouldn't be able to tell the difference. Not that I'd be in a dark room with Harold's testicles in the first place."

I watch the color drain from her face as she contemplates the possibility she may have inadvertently married a woman, and how this revelation could affect her social status. After a moment she gives it one last stab: "I've seen him without a shirt. Even if he were flat-chested I'd be able to tell if—"

Hearing my name on the intercom, I cut her off. "Sorry Gail, I've gotta run. I didn't mean to imply Harold has a normal woman's bosom. By every possible standard he appears to be a man. Except for...you know...his vagina."

"Are you saying Harold's a *lesbian?*"

The intercom loudly announces my heart patient's waiting for me in Exam Room 4. "Duty calls," I say. "We'll chat soon."

Gail grabs my hand, places it on her boob, kisses it: my hand, not her boob. "I want to see you in three days," she says. "In a more private setting."

"That sounds promising."

She says, "In the meantime, I don't suppose you'd write me a scrip?"

"I could if I happened to bring my pad. Let's see." I remove my hand from her tit, reach into the pocket of my lab coat, and pull out a thermometer. "Shit!"

"What's wrong?"

"Some asshole's got my pen!"

She frowns. "Is that supposed to be funny?"

"Yes."

"Well, it isn't."

"Sorry. I'll make it up to you."

"Promise?"

"Yup."

She stands on her tiptoes, kisses my cheek and whispers in my ear: "Until then, handsome."

Then she sets her jaw and stomps off to see Harold, leaving me to wish I could be there when she rips his gown open, grabs his dick and starts pulling and tugging to see if it's prosthetic. I hold my laughter till she disappears behind his door, then head to Room 4 to meet the heart patient who's about to change the course of my life.

Chapter 4

I'M NOT SURPRISED Judson Bray got an examination room moments after his arrival: he reeks of wealth, and arrived complaining of chest pains. Even without his financial credentials he'd get a fast track to an exam room, since heart issues mean you deserve to be here.

Bray's hooked up to all the machines you'd see on a high budget TV show, and since this shit costs his insurance company a fortune, I pretend to study the monitors for several minutes prior to introducing myself. Then I ask about his medical history, and read the comments written by the Emergency Nurse and her minions.

Mr. Bray has no history of heart attack, but sports two stents from a percutaneous coronary intervention he underwent four years ago. Though he appears healthy as a horse, who knows what evil lurks within those arteries? I question him about the blood-thinners and anti-cholesterol meds he takes, and ask what made him visit our ER this afternoon.

As he starts talking, I keep my expression neutral and tune him out while contemplating the most effective way to kill him, should our relationship sour. It's not personal, it's something I do with all the adult patients I encounter in the hospital. Not that I've actually killed *scores* of them, or even close to that number. That would be criminal, right?

I've killed...about a dozen.

Approximately.

I mean, I don't go around carving notches on my stethoscope, so if you're asking for the exact number I'd have to count them up. Would you like me to?

Okay, hang on a sec...

Fifteen.

Don't let it make you nervous. These weren't random patients, and weren't even *my* patients, since as I said earlier, I only get infants and children. The adults I killed were people—or relatives of people—who treated me badly at some point in my life. Like the guys who bullied me in junior high, or the ones who stole my girlfriends. Or the parents who wouldn't let their daughters date me. Or the girl who cheated on me when we were supposedly going steady. Or the woman who laughed in my face at the fundraiser when I asked her for a date. Or the guy who sold me a bad car and wouldn't take it back at a fair price. They're the ones who...

Well, you get the idea, and you're probably aware I'm referring to hundreds of potential victims, and since I've only killed 15, you can see I've barely scratched the surface. My biggest problem has been that most of the people who have wronged me—or their relatives—haven't received treatment in my hospital.

Yet.

But they're on my LIST.

Judson's not on my LIST, but he might be the close friend or relative of someone who *is*. Which brings up a good point: if you're in my hospital and I'm questioning you about people you might know, it's not because I'm being congenial. It's because I'm looking for a connection between you and someone on my LIST.

You might think it's difficult keeping up with all these future victims, but all I really need is my laptop and a keyword search application. I enter Sally Gaither's name, and whenever something happens in her life it pops up in my email. Maybe she married Benson Rayburn, or moved to Clark County, or maybe she attended a lavish party with her best friend, Toni Stevens. When those new names pop up they go into the hospital database, to be cross-referenced with our patient list for possible matches.

I doubt Judson's related to Sally Gaither, but since they both went to Princeton, I take the time to ask if he happens to know her.

He doesn't.

Sally's on my LIST because she was directly responsible for my nickname *The Fly*, back in seventh grade. We were at a party, and she was given the choice to kiss me or eat a dead fly, and...

She chose the fly.

At the time, I was relieved she didn't want to kiss me, since the whole grade would have made fun of us. But when she chose the fly that became my nickname. And at every party for the next two years, girls were given the choice to do something really gross or kiss *The Fly*. And of course they chose to do the gross thing, because even if they would've *preferred* to kiss me they wouldn't have dared. Because kissing *The Fly* would be social suicide, as in: "*Omigod! You kissed The Fly? You are so gross! You should kill yourself!*"

If you called me *The Fly*, or drew pictures of *The Fly* on the bathroom walls, or refused to kiss me—you can safely assume you're on the LIST. And if you don't happen to be a patient in my hospital I'm perfectly willing to punish the people you love. Like if Sally's husband or daughter checks in someday I'll know because they'll list their next-of-kin and emergency contacts on the admittance forms, and a program on my computer automatically collects those names and screens them for possible matches.

Eventually, you and your loved ones will either get sick or have an accident. And although I can only get to you if you're a patient in my hospital, you might be surprised how effectively the six degrees of separation works. If fifteen matches in the six years I've been here seems like a small number to you, remember the immortal title of the second-best Stones song ever recorded: *Time Is on My Side*. Because time *is* on my side, and the older these people get, the more likely they'll suffer an illness or accident.

As Judson drones on about his chest pains and how they affected him today, I come to the conclusion he could best be killed (a) immediately by injecting a lethal agent into his IV drip, or (b) over days by replacing one of his statin pills with an identical-looking herbal supplement that causes fatal interactions with his antiplatelet medication.

You're probably thinking I'd get caught because hospitals strictly monitor dangerous drugs. Well, they do, but their main focus is regulating addictive drugs like ketamine, OxyContin, Vicodin, morphine, and the like. But you know what's easy? Killing a patient with a drug that's supposed to save him. Like digoxin, which is used to help regulate heart rhythm.

Having said all that, the simplest way to kill Judson would be to admit him as a patient and keep him here long enough to contract an HAI (hospital-acquired infection). Because more people die from hospital infections each year than from breast cancer, auto accidents, and AIDS...*combined!*

These infections are caused by bacteria, fungi, viruses, and parasites that enter your body through an orifice, incision, or an existing wound or cut.

What's that you say? You don't *have* a wound or cut?

No problem, we'll give you one!

Ever been prepped for a procedure? When our nurse shaves that small area of hair from your groin she'll probably break the skin just enough to allow bacteria to gain entry. The cuts are microscopic. You won't see or feel them, but they can kill you.

Or maybe we'll give you one of the dozens of drugs that make you itch, and while sleeping in your hospital bed you'll subconsciously scratch that ingrown hair on your thigh.

Two days later you're dead, and no one knows why.

Of course, the antibiotics we give you can save your life, but they'll also put you at risk for contracting C-diff, which can give you life-threatening diarrhea. Ever had a really bad case of diarrhea? Imagine diarrhea so bad you actually *die* from it!

That said, 52% of hospital-acquired infections could be eliminated if doctors, nurses, and orderlies would simply remember to wash their hands before entering each room. But you know who has the guts to say, "*Wash your fucking hands, doctor?*"

No one.

So the patients keep dying.

Judson Bray has excellent insurance, so I order a full round of tests and inform him he'll be our guest for at least eight hours.

He asks me to call his wife.

I tell him there's no reason he can't personally call her, since it'll take at least 30 minutes to schedule his first test.

He says if I call her she'll take it seriously.

I'm a little surprised his wife won't take it seriously if he calls from a hospital emergency room prior to undergoing tests for a possible heart attack, but I *am* curious about her. Is she a trophy wife? Probably. Might she be willing to trade sex for drugs at some point in the future? Unlikely, but you never know for sure about such things, which is why I pride myself on keeping an open mind when it comes to sex, drugs, and rock n' roll.

I dig through the plastic bag that holds Judson's clothing and personal items, seeking his cell phone, but locate his house and car keys first. The car key's so cool I have to ask what type of Porsche he has.

He smiles. "918 Spyder. Ever drive one?"

"I've never even *seen* one! Not in person, anyway."

"You should try it sometime. It's unlike anything you've ever experienced."

"I'm more of a Volvo sedan-type guy," I lie, pocketing his keys. I locate his phone, then enter his field of vision. He says, "Just press the first name on the favorites list."

"Ellie Bray?"

He nods. "I really appreciate this, Doc. Ellie considers me a hypochondriac, but if the ER doctor calls her, she'll take it seriously."

"Are you *purposely* trying to scare her?"

"Uh..." He looks at me like he may have said too much. But I quickly reassure him I'm on his team, saying: "Because if you want, I can scare the *shit* out of this bitch!"

He grins.

I click her name. As the number rings, Ellie's picture comes up, and I'm pleased to see she's smoking hot. I angle the phone to Judson and whisper, "Wow!"

He nods.

"How old?" I ask.

"Twenty-eight."

Ellie answers with a voice heavily lubricated with inconvenience: "I'm really busy, Judson. What do you want?"

To which I respond, "This isn't Judson, Mrs. Bray. I'm Dr. Gideon Box, and I'm calling from the Emergency Room of Shit Fuck Hospital." (Our hospital obviously isn't named Shit Fuck, and that's not the name I gave her. But since I've already admitted I kill people here I'd rather not incriminate myself further. You understand, don't you?)

Ellie, suddenly serious, says, "What's happened?"

And I say...

Chapter 5

"I'M AFRAID THERE'S been an incident."

"A *what? Omigod!* What's happened?"

"We think your husband may have suffered a heart attack." Judson's giving me a thumbs-up, so I add, "He's doing
as well as can be expected, but I've got him under close observation. We're going to run some tests, but you should
know we're taking this quite seriously."

"What do you mean?" she says.

"There's a distinct possibility his condition could deteriorate at any moment."

As I say these words I notice Judson's laughing his ass
off, though quietly, since he's holding a pillow over his nose
and mouth. Which reminds me that suffocation by pillow
would be the fourth easiest way to kill him.

Would it surprise you to hear that patients occasionally
smother their critically ill spouses with hospital pillows?
Here's how that goes down: when a patient is critically ill

and suffering terribly but won't die, critical care nurses have been known to place pillows in the spouse's hands and give them a knowing look before leaving the room, closing the door, walking away, and waiting for the alarm to sound.

Ellie starts to ask me something specific, but I interrupt her, saying, "I'm sorry, I can't talk right now. But if you'll come to the hospital we can update you on his condition."

"Thank you, Doctor, I'm on my way. Uh...please take care of him, okay?"

"Of course."

"Give him the finest care possible. Whatever he needs. Money's no object."

"Thank you, Mrs. Bray. We'll do all we can for him."

I hang up and look at Judson, who's shaking his head, saying, "You're the *man*! Holy shit! You even had *me* going!"

"Don't get too cheerful, Mr. Bray. Everything I told her is possible at this point."

That sobers him up enough to allow me to ask a series of "lifestyle" questions that are so intrusive and personal you'd never believe a total stranger would answer them. It helps that I'm a doctor, because people will tell a doctor things they wouldn't tell their spouses or best friends. Plus, Judson's totally up my ass, convinced I'm his friend and confidante.

After getting every last piece of information I want, I leave his room and get my medical bag from the locker so if anyone sees me slipping out the back entrance they'll assume I'm tending to one of my critically ill patients. The staff has been warned this could happen at any time, and that my actual patients take precedent over my "community service" punishment.

I check to make sure none of the staff members are loitering near the exit that leads to the doctor's parking area. My plan is to...

Wait! —Is that Nurse Jennifer?

It is!

She's standing by the far corridor, motioning me to approach her.

I smile to myself. It took her a little longer than expected, but after thinking it over she obviously decided furthering her career is worth the small concession of having dinner with me. I can only dream what other concessions she might be willing to make in the name of career advancement.

As I make my way toward her, she surprises me by whispering, "Follow me quickly. And don't call attention to yourself."

As Jennifer leads me to an exam room I'm thinking blow job. But when she opens the door I see two terrified young men—a physician's assistant and a med student—standing over a patient who's lying face-down on a gurney with a syringe sticking out of the middle of his back.

I frown. Not because I give a shit about the patient or the ineptitude of our hospital's future doctors, but because whatever this is, it's neither blow job nor dinner date with Nurse Jennifer.

"Is he alive?" I ask.

"Yeah," the PA says. "But I think we might have paralyzed him."

The med student starts to explain how it happened, but I wave him off. I know exactly how it happened, and trust me, you don't want to know *all* the details of what they've done to this poor guy. So I'll sum it up this way: when young doctors and med students get you unconscious in an Emergency Room, they sometimes come to the conclusion it's a perfect place to practice their technique. The PA was walking the med student through a routine procedure, and this being his first time, the med student jammed the syringe into the backbone so deeply that attempting to remove it forcibly could cause the needle to break. If that happens, the PA and med student will be involved in an *incident*, which could lead to a *report*, which could lead to all sorts of terrible things. But if the PA and med student can get a *doctor* to remove the syringe, he becomes their scapegoat. If something goes horribly wrong with this situation, the liability falls on me.

If I had any doubts how badly Nurse Jennifer dislikes me, I now stand convinced. Because out of the half-dozen doctors milling around the ER she took the time to choose *me* for this particular duty.

Nice try, Jenn, but this ain't my first rodeo.

I grab my cell phone and start shooting pictures before anyone can stop me. I've got both guys standing by the body, and Nurse Jennifer in front of me. Then I press the record button and shoot a live video while recapping exactly what happened.

When I end the recording I surprise them by saying, "I can fix this, but you'll owe me."

The PA says, "What about the video?"

"I'll hang onto it."

The MS looks at Nurse Jennifer. "What about her?"

"She's the wild card."

"What do you mean?"

"She can report you for what you did, but since she hasn't, I expect she's waiting to see if I'm going to report you. If I don't, she'll have power over me for helping you participate in a cover up."

The PA says, "Jennifer? This stuff happens all the time. It was a terrible accident, but no one intended the guy to get hurt."

Jennifer says nothing.

The MS says, "Dr. Box can save our *careers*."

The PA says, "You're not going to report us, are you?"

She looks at me.

I shrug. "I can help them or report them. Your choice."

"Actually," she says, "It's *your* choice, doctor."

The PA glares at her. Then says, "It's our word against hers."

"Relax," Jennifer says. "I *do* want something from the two of you, but it's a very small request. I'm new here, and I'll obviously make some mistakes. I'll only ask that you look out for me whenever possible."

"What do you mean?" the PA asks.

"It means if you see I've done something wrong you'll tell me, and help me fix it. It means if you hear something bad about me you'll tell something good I did to help balance it out."

He shrugs. "You're gorgeous. We'd do that anyway."

"Like I said, it's a small request." She looks at me and says, "As for you?"

"Yeah?"

"I'll simply ask you to stop hitting on me."

"That's it?"

"That's it. However..."

I laugh. "Here it comes!"

She says, "If you really believe I have potential as a nurse, I'd appreciate it if you don't do anything to hurt my chances of staying here."

"Like yelling at you in front of the team?"

She smiles. "You can yell all you want. But only if I actually do something wrong."

I smile back. "I really do like you, Jennifer."

"I know. But try not to, okay?"

"Okay."

I turn my attention to the patient and carefully twist the hypodermic needle between my fingertips. Right, then left, then right, like I'm working a combination lock, except that while spinning it I apply just enough pressure to work it free without breaking the needle. Then I treat the wound and leave them with a recommendation to study the anatomy of the backbone tonight so they'll understand why I knew they hadn't paralyzed him.

Then I leave the room, sneak out of the ER, enter the main hospital, and exit through the door where I know the security camera's broken. I know because I got a blow job from a grateful patient's mother outside this very door last Monday night, and no one from security called to blackmail me.

Why would they blackmail me, you ask?

Because the guys who work the cameras on this shift are notorious pill junkies who constantly try to catch me doing something wrong. They focus on me because of my past transgressions. On several occasions I had to score some heavy shit for them to keep my job and medical license. At the moment, we're even. And though they're working against me, we have a good relationship: as long as I have the ability to hook them up with drugs, they'll cover for me.

Chapter 6

I CAN'T JUST press the unlock button and climb into Judson's Porsche.

I have to make sure I'm not seen by hospital staff or parking lot cameras. So if his car is among the first three rows...

It's not.

This is a happy surprise, because if I were Judson—even if I thought I was having a heart attack—I wouldn't park my 918 Spyder this far from the entrance.

It takes less than a minute to locate the car, scan the area, climb in, and close the door. With that done, let me tell you about this fucking car! For starters, sticker price is $930,000! Standard features include a 4.6L V-8 608hp engine, 7-speed auto-shift manual transmission with overdrive, 20-inch magnesium wheels, ABS and driveline traction control, all-wheel drive.

Would you be surprised to know I can afford this car and 100 more just like it?

It's true.

The hospital pays me a fortune for what I do, but not *that* type of money! The extra hundred million I'm referring to came from an off-the-books surgery I performed 18 months ago on a billionaire assassin's key employee. The assassin, Donovan Creed...

Well, it's a long story. Let's just say he needed me, and I restored his employee's ability to walk. In return, he paid me a hundred million dollars. As for Creed: that is one scary-ass motherfucker!

I fire up Judson's car and exit the parking lot with a clear destination in mind:

His house.

Why? Because he and Ellie won't be there, and I know how to get past his security gates.

How, you say?

Simple: When talking to Judson about his car I mentioned my car has buttons on the visor that are supposed to open the front gate and garage door, but I could never get them to work. He told me his work fine.

Thanks, Judson!

And due to the intrusive "lifestyle" questions I asked, I happen to know that Judson's only child, daughter Chelsea, is away at college, and that Emma Watson—his housekeeper, not the actress—leaves at 6 p.m. each day. By the time I arrive it'll be seven, which means I'll have the house to myself.

I love going through people's houses, especially rich people's. Since Judson and Ellie live 45 minutes from

Manhattan, on twelve acres of land, and aren't part of a gated community, their home will make a perfect hideaway I can use when they're out of town (I "collect" these types of residences for personal use, make copies of their house keys, treat their homes and belongings as if my own, and monitor their lives through information-gathering phone calls disguised as doctor-patient follow ups. Example: after chatting about a patient's general health I might ask, "Do you guys have any fun trips planned for the holidays? ...Oh really? That sounds wonderful! Where are you going? ...great choice! How long will you get to stay there? —Wow, good for you!")

Of course, housekeepers and kids can spoil my plans quickly. I expect Emma and Chelsea will both want to use Judson and Ellie's cars while they're out of town, use their swimming pool, eat their food, and steal some of their valuables. I want to do all those things too, but unlike Emma and Chelsea, I'll also use his home phone to call hookers and drug dealers for personal visits (Don't think me crass. I'm referring to call girls and dealers of the highest quality, not street people).

Although I lifted Judson's address from his medical records, I don't need to enter it into his navigation system since it's already there, listed as "home" on his settings. I'd love to take this puppy full-throttle on the Interstate, but since getting arrested for speeding in a stolen car could stain my resume, I reluctantly follow the navigation system's pleasant-sounding voice at a lawful speed till it takes me to Judson's mildly secluded 12,000 square-foot home in the gorgeous community of Purchase, in Harrison, New York.

Purchase, with its winding roads and abundant wooded areas, happens to be the 25th wealthiest neighborhood in the entire United States. I know this from comments made at a recent fundraising party that was held less than a mile from this very residence.

I enter the gates and turn into the driveway without hesitating, but have to press three garage door buttons until I find one with an empty bay. I pull in, press the buttons to close the doors, climb out of the Porsche, and survey the garage, noting two luxury cars, the Porsche, and the empty bay where Ellie's car would be if she were here.

I wonder what type of car she typically drives, and can't believe I didn't think to ask Judson, since it would have been fun to spot her racing toward the hospital in the opposite direction on I-287, even as I headed to her place to snoop through her underwear drawer.

The door key works. As expected, Ellie didn't take the time to set the alarm before leaving, which saves me a frantic search for the code and safe word. But I would have found them, because crazy as it sounds, I've never broken into a house and not been able to do so. That's because people are predictable, and in my experience the code and safe word are almost always written on the inside, front, or back cover of the alarm instruction booklet, which is almost always located in the top or side drawer of the built-in desk in the kitchen.

The door from garage to house puts me in a small entrance area with two bench seats and numerous cubbies the Brays use for storing coats, shoes, umbrellas, and sports equipment, and this area opens to a hallway. Looking left, I see the laundry room and a half-bath.

First opening to the right is a small room with a desk and computer, which probably belongs to Ellie. On impulse, I open the top left drawer to find a number of instruction manuals for various appliances, as well as *the burglar alarm instruction manual* with—you guessed it—the alarm code on the back cover, scrawled in ink!

I memorize the four-digit code as well as the safe word written below it, then walk the hallway. Ignoring the pantry on the left, I enter the kitchen on the right, and immediately curb-appraise the thick granite countertops, custom cabinets, and top-flight appliances at over a quarter million dollars. I inventory the contents of their refrigerator, freezer, and cabinets, then stroll through their oversized den and spend several minutes studying the photos on the walls, tables, and countertops, and come to the conclusion Ellie Bray is hotter than a West Texas bonfire in August (Unlike her 18-year-old daughter, Chelsea, whose DNA clearly originated from one of Judson's former, less attractive wives).

Walking through the dining and living rooms, I marvel at the high ceilings, exquisite crown molding, elegant faux finishes, and impeccable decor. Now, just past the foyer, I inspect the massive wet bar and note the complete absence of wines above table-grade, which tells me I'm certain to find an impressive wine cellar in the basement. I'll save that treasure for my next visit, when I'll have endless hours to check labels and sample the stock.

Next stop is Judson's ultra-paneled office, where I expect to find the locked drawer where he keeps his checkbook and gun. But to my surprise there are no locked drawers, and no gun. I leave his office, briefly poke my head in the opulent powder room, then enter the master bedroom and search their nightstand drawers, but find no condoms, lube, or sex toys.

Not to worry. If Ellie's hiding a dildo or other sex toys, I'll find them. I'm something of an expert, having found them in other homes in all the following places:

In cookie jars.

Under mattresses.

In pillow cases.

Behind headboards.

In Tampon boxes.

In vases.

In bags of frozen vegetables in the freezer.

In old handbags.

In hats and hat boxes.

In old tennis shoes.

Under the chair cushion in the bedroom.

In cereal boxes in the pantry.

In the small triangle of space behind the photo of grandma catty-cornered in the bookcase.

And my personal favorite: in stuffed animals, where the homeowners cut a slit in the fabric and used Velcro to keep it closed!

It'll be fun to hunt for them, but if they're not in Judson or Ellie's closets, I'll probably save that quest for my next visit.

Judson's closet reveals a stash of cash, two loaded hand-guns, and a hunting knife. I count the cash and come up with $2,860.00, which seems an odd amount that he probably hasn't memorized. In other words, if I took a hundred bucks he probably wouldn't know. I punch the amount into the Notes app on my cell phone so I can compare it with the amount I find on my next visit. While I've got the app open, I go ahead and punch in their alarm code and safe word.

Now, to Ellie's closet...

Chapter 7

ELLIE'S CLOSET IS *huge!*

Normally I wouldn't go into detail, but this is really special. To my left, there are four racks of dresses (more than 100!), and eight racks of jeans, blouses, skirts, and stretchy workout clothes. The second wall features a padded bench seat, a large window, a six-foot-tall mirror, and a ladder she can climb to reach the higher areas. The third is floor-to-ceiling with wooden built-ins: cubicles, cubbies, and racks for shoes, boots, belts, and handbags. Want me to count them for you?

Okay: There are...42 pairs of boots, 78 pairs of shoes, 19 belts, 7 hat boxes, and 37 handbags, all of the highest-quality leather.

Yes, I said *thirty-seven* handbags!

What surprises me is what I don't find: a safe.

The focal point of Ellie's closet is a giant, custom-made dresser positioned in the center, standing five feet high, six feet wide, four feet deep, with—astonishingly—15 drawers! Want me to open them?

Of course you do!

From top left to right, the first drawer contains a half-dozen bra pads and something called "petals" which appear to be flesh-colored pads she apparently places over her twat so she won't have to wear panties. There are also breast petals for the no-bra look, and foot petals, to cushion her feet when wearing high heels. Next drawer is *very* nice costume jewelry, and I assume the third drawer contains the *real* jewelry, since she keeps it locked.

No problem, I'm sure to find the key in one of the other drawers, under a pile of clothes. My guess? Her underwear drawer.

Second row, left to right: approximately 20 *more* bra pads, and 8 designer sunglasses, in fancy cases. Middle drawer: several boxes with more costume jewelry, including several pieces of real gold with small diamonds that apparently aren't nice enough to keep locked in the top right-hand drawer. Next drawer: Panties. I count...35 in assorted colors. Most are XS, others, S. All but 8 are thongs. She also has 4 boy shorts, and two items I can't figure out that resemble black headbands. I steal one so I can look it up on the Internet and learn how it's supposed to be worn.

Third row, left drawer: more bra pads! You'd swear this woman must have five pairs of tits! There's also a bag filled with my specialty: prescription drugs. According to the labels, nearly all have outlived their expiration dates, which means, sadly, Ellie isn't an addict.

Third row, middle drawer is bathing suits and...wait. I hear a tapping sound, coming from the one room I haven't checked:

The master bath.

I immediately stop what I'm doing, stand perfectly still; listen.

There it is again: a tapping sound. Followed by a raspy wheeze.

The kind a person makes.

My senses switch to high alert, and my heart starts pounding so hard I can practically feel it slamming against my rib cage. As the blood rushes through my body, feeding my brain, I hear a "sparkly" sound in my inner ear that's sort of like white noise. I feel nauseous. Lightheaded. Alive! Everything goes to slow motion, and when I try to walk it's like the floor is covered in wet cement.

But I manage to move my feet, and after the first few sloggy steps, I find myself in the hallway. To the right is the master bath. To the left? Well, I could retrace my steps, make my way to the garage, and hope to exit without being seen....

But you know me:

I have to know who's here.

It's almost certainly Emma the housekeeper. After hearing about Judson, Ellie probably asked her to stay late, in case...

Actually, I can't think of any reason why Emma would have to stay late. Also, there were no cars in the driveway, and I can't imagine Emma Watson drives one of the luxury cars I saw in the garage.

I hear another faint tap and wonder what the chances are that Judson's daughter, Chelsea, happened to come home from school shortly after Ellie left for the hospital?

My mind conjures thoughts of Chelsea making a surprise visit home, only to find her dad and stepmother gone. Not knowing he's in the hospital, I picture her taking a shower in their bathroom, which is probably far nicer than the one in her upstairs bedroom. By now she's freshly showered, wearing earbuds, listening to music playing so loudly she hasn't heard me moving through the house. The tapping could be her fingernails, tapping against the marble countertop, as she sits at Ellie's makeup area in the master bathroom, preparing to apply makeup.

I put all this together in the space of two seconds, which gives me the courage to turn right and follow the hall to the master bathroom, a distance of ten feet, a journey I make creeping cat-like, one careful step at a time.

And sure enough, I do see someone in there. A female, on the floor.

Not Chelsea, or Emma the housekeeper, but shockingly...Ellie Bray!

It's absolutely Ellie, and she's lying sideways on the bathroom floor, angled toward the hallway, eyes glazed, staring straight ahead, one arm extended, the other clutching her neck.

The beautiful Ellie, whose upper torso and face is surrounded by a pool of blood.

I move closer, and see that her throat has been slashed from ear to ear.

And though she was tapping the fingernail of her extended arm against the marble floor just seconds ago, she isn't tapping now.

She's dead.

And yet...

Chapter 8

I'M THE POLAR opposite of that kid in the creepy Bruce Willis movie. Where he used to *see* dead people, I bring them back to life.

And just to clarify, though I told you Ellie Bray was dead, she's *freshly*-dead, which is quite different from being *permanently* dead.

I won't insult you by claiming that over the next 40 minutes I ran to the garage, grabbed my medical bag from Judson's car, raced back to the bathroom, removed my clothes to avoid transferring blood evidence, brought Ellie back to life, stitched her up, cleaned my bloody footprints and body prints from the floor, then showered and put my clothes back on—

—But that's exactly what happened.

You're skeptical.

I get that.

But here's what *I* know that *you* don't: it's extremely difficult to kill a person with a knife. That's why you often hear about victims having 30, 40, or even 50 stab wounds. On TV they always use that high number to explain the murder was a crime of passion. That's often true, but an even better explanation is: *that's how many stab wounds it took to make the victim die!*

That said, Ellie's attacker did, in fact, succeed in killing her with a single slice. By the time I got my clothes off she'd been without a discernable pulse for close to two minutes. But two minutes does not a dead woman make. As a general rule of thumb, once the pulse ceases, you've got four to six minutes to get adequate blood flow to the body and brain cells before death or permanent brain damage ensues.

You're probably wondering how I performed mouth-to-mouth on a woman whose throat was slashed.

I didn't.

Nor did I reach into my physician's bag and pull out defibrillation paddles, yell "Clear!" and shock her back to life like they do on TV, which, by the way, is the only place paddles can bring people back to life after they've flat-lined.

I almost hate to tell you how I "miraculously" brought her back to life, since you must be thinking of me as a god or super hero right now.

I rolled her over.

Simply rolled her over so I could work on her, and...she started breathing!

Crazy, right?

Of course, once she was on her back I realized her wound hadn't been made by a professional killer, or she'd have died within three minutes of the attack. More likely, this is the work of an amateur, and she's been lying here at least a half hour.

Saving Ellie did not require divine intervention. I simply administered a drug cocktail and used chest compressions to circulate both her blood and my medicine through her body. That, and the additional comorbid factors including her age, level of fitness, runner's heartbeat, and of course dumb luck—combined to render my bathroom surgery a temporary success.

Temporary, because her life is literally hanging by a thread, and therein lies my problem: if I call 911, they'll have my voice on tape. Call me pessimistic, but I don't think the police will be impressed to learn I saved her life *after* stealing Judson's car, breaking into their home, and going through their closets.

Do *you* have any ideas for me?

I'm serious, 'cause I've got zip. I mean, how would *you* explain to the cops that—instead of calling 911—you decided to personally work on Ellie, and while doing so, you compromised, contaminated, and manipulated the crime scene? And while you're at it, perhaps you can tell me how to explain why, after patching her up, I left her lying here on the floor while I took a shower, ten feet away?

I shouldn't have rolled her over. If I hadn't, she'd be dead.

But I *did* roll her over, and now I'm stuck in a situation: if I don't call for emergency help, she'll die, and soon, and I'll be guilty of murder.

Yeah, I know what you're thinking: the smart move would have been to leave her where I found her. I could have gone through the house, wiped away my fingerprints. I could have driven back to the hospital and pretended none of this ever happened.

But I have this character flaw: when I see someone freshly dead that I didn't personally kill, I try to save them.

Okay, so I can do one of three things: call 911, tell them what to expect when they get here, and wait for them. This, of course is the *right* thing to do. I'd have to pay the price for what I've done, but the mitigating circumstances of saving Ellie's life—if she survives—might cause a judge to go easy on me later on. Second, I could do all the above, but disguise my voice, flee the scene, and hope for the best. And third, I could try to remember every surface I touched with my hands, wipe them clean, flee the scene, and hope no one can figure out which surgeon happened to show up and save Ellie's life. But the problem with this is there are less than 20 living surgeons who can stitch a person the way I just did, and since half of them reside outside the country, what are the chances the cops will figure out it was me?

That's right, 100%.

Unless...

Chapter 9

EVERYONE ANSWERS TO someone.

I don't care who you are or what you do for a living, there's at least one phone call you'll always take. Maybe it's your doctor, with your test results; or your attorney, with your settlement or plea deal. Or maybe it's your boss, your bookie, or your drug dealer. Or your mother, sister, husband, or wife. Maybe it's one of your kids. I bet 20 people can call the President of the United States any time, day or night, and he has to answer.

The reason I'm bringing this up, I have three people like this. Three whose calls I can't ignore. And since my phone's ringing right now and caller ID says it's one of them (Donovan Creed, the government assassin-slash-contract killer) I take the call and try to sound casual: "Hey Donovan, What's up?"

"Everything okay, Doc?"

"Yes, of course."

"You're sure about that?"

Creed's the one who paid me the hundred million I told you about earlier. He's also unstable as hell. Like other hit men, Creed will kill you for a fee, but he also might kill you because it's Tuesday. Whoever you are, wherever you are: if you woke up this morning it's because Creed didn't decide to kill you last night.

Think I'm embellishing?

He once explained, to my professional satisfaction, three different ways he's killed people with a single sheet of typing paper...

In the same building, in the same night.

"Everything's great!" I say.

We're quiet till he says something that makes my blood run cold, to which I respond, "Of course."

He says, "Excellent. I'll be in touch."

We hang up, and I look at Ellie's body on the floor and marvel how just moments ago my biggest problem was what to do about her. But compared to what Creed just said, this Ellie thing doesn't even rise to the level of being an inconvenience.

What he said was: "I need a favor."

Chapter 10

CREED'S FAVORS ARE legendary. If you owe him one
and he calls it in, you do it or die. While that might sound
melodramatic, the reality is far worse. Because it's *how* he
kills you that makes the difference. And if you *disappoint*
him, well...you don't want to disappoint him.

"I'll be in touch," he said.

What does *that* mean?

It means he's put me on notice.

I look at Ellie. She's stable, but suffering. Yes, I should
call an ambulance, but I don't. Instead, I grab a towel and go
through the house and wipe every surface, light switch and
knob I remember touching, and hope to hell I got them all. I
try not to think about how if I become a suspect the police
will be able to track my cell phone to within several yards of
this very location at the time of the *incident*. That, plus the
stitch work, would do me in.

Since I can't control those issues, I concentrate on what I *can* do: unlock the front and back doors, grab my medical bag, climb into Judson's Porsche, and head to the nearest tavern. I walk in, sit at the bar, order a drink, start sipping it, and a beautiful young lady takes the spot beside me and says, "If I told you my name was Jackie Fish, would you believe me?"

Since I already told you how this encounter went, up to the part where she pretended to be a cop and I agreed to take her to Inspiration Point, I'll start with what's happening right now, in real time: We're leaving the bar, walking to Judson's car. It's nearly dusk, which means we've got about an hour of daylight left. I ask if she's got a cell phone.

"Who doesn't?" she says.

"I want you to call 911 and tell them to send an ambulance to the address I'm about to give you."

I look at Jackie, expecting her to protest. But she says, "I'll want to make the call from inside the car, privately."

"That's fine, but I need to hear everything you say."

"Okay, but you'll have to stand outside the car and face the other way. Otherwise, you'll make me self-conscious."

"Okay."

She gets in the car and lowers the window so I can hear. I stand ten feet away and listen as she calls 911, gives the operator Ellie's address, tells them the front door is unlocked, and tells them to send an ambulance immediately. Then, as instructed, she hangs up.

I smile. Whatever else happens tonight, Jackie's already been a huge help to me in four ways: one, we may have saved Ellie's life. Two, I'm about to be laid by a hot chick who—three—just became my alibi. And four, the 911 operator has Jackie's voice on tape, not only making the call, but identifying an emergency situation and directing emergency personnel to the address where they'll find a woman dying on the floor of the master bathroom. To put it another way, if Ellie dies, Jackie has lowered me from prime suspect to possible suspect!

I get in the car and follow her directions to Inspiration Point, which turns out to be the East Coast version of a scenic overlook, except that there are lights all over the place. If their presence is meant to discourage lovemaking, it's not affecting Jackie Fish, who's rubbing my crotch with such enthusiasm you'd think she expects a genie to pop out and grant her three wishes. I lie back, feel my eyes roll up into my head, and apparently make some sort of moaning sound, because she admonishes me, saying, "Dude! Act like you've done this before!"

"Oh. Sorry."

"Let's get your pants off."

"Good idea!"

I unfasten my belt, unzip my pants, then do that thing where you lift your butt off the seat, arch your back, and try to shimmy your pants down, but there's not enough leg room to work with, so I lower my body, move the car seat back as far as it'll go, and try again.

Jackie waits patiently while I perform these gyrations, and when I'm finally naked from the waist down with my pants just below my knees, she stares at my erection with wide eyes—as if it holds the secrets of the universe. Then she looks up at me and smiles.

I smile back.

She points at my manhood and shifts into roll-play, pretending to be a little girl: "What's *that*, Doctor?"

"My penis," I say, proudly.

"Wow!" she says. "I've never seen one of *those* before!"

"*Never?*"

"No sir."

"What do you think of it, young lady?"

"It looks a lot like a man's cock, only smaller."

I frown.

She says, "Oh, goodness, Doctor. It's shriveling up! I wouldn't have believed it could actually get *smaller*, but...omigod, it looks like an *acorn*! Whatever should we *do?*"

"Look. I didn't come all this way to be insulted."

She shifts back to her real voice: "If you didn't want to be insulted, you shouldn't have brought this penis to the party. It's like opening a bucket of farts in an elevator. I've seen *newborns* with bigger dicks."

"I've never had any complaints."

"Nor would I expect complaints from hookers and chloroform victims."

I'm sensing a definite shift in her mood. Moments ago she was all over me. Now she hates me. It can't be the size of my dick...unless her previous lovers were circus animals.

"Speaking of hookers," I say, "perhaps I should mention you've been paid in advance to render a service."

"True. And I'm seriously considering giving you a refund, and extra cash for a penis implant."

I look at what's left of my erection and wonder if I should pack it in. Then Jackie flicks my dick with her finger

68

a couple of times, and I can't decide if she's trying to humil-iate me or make me bigger. Either way, she's still here, and that singular fact gives me hope. As for being humiliated, I'm an older guy, so I expect a certain amount of humilia-tion in any sexual relationship. I'm that guy who—in the middle of the actual fucking—often sees my conquest crying. Not because she'll hate herself in the morning, but because she hates herself right *then*.

"You promised sex," I remind her. "But if you're having second thoughts, I'll settle for a blow job."

Jackie looks at me like I'd just said the third-craziest thing ever (the first two being Kanye West, who said: "I'm a god," and, "I'm a genius.") Then she says, "Could you even *accept* a blow job from me, knowing the very thought of it makes me want to vomit?"

"Of course."

"And if I *do* vomit?"

"I'll deal with it."

"You're *that* desperate?"

"No, but I'm invested."

"You know what you are? A *pig* of a man! You *disgust* me. How does *that* make you feel?"

"I feel you should say whatever you need to in order to get through the experience. It may not be fun or easy, but you can do this. Others have."

"You're insane."

"Yes, and you're rude. But let's not allow our shortcom-ings to interfere with what could turn out to be a perfectly good blow job. Or fuck, if you'd prefer."

"I'd prefer death," she says, melodramatically.

I think I understand her change of heart. Her reason for wanting to be here had nothing to do with a bucket list that included having sex in a Porsche. More likely, she was planning to meet someone here, and he stood her up, or hasn't arrived yet. I'm guessing Jackie left her husband and planned to meet her lover here, but got dropped off at the tavern, six miles away. Needing to get here as fast as possible, she said whatever she had to, and now she's humiliating me, hoping I'll have too much pride to accept the sex she offered.

But that's a false hope, because I'm an older guy who likes younger pussy. If I had any pride I'd *never* get laid.

The other possibility is Jackie's on the fence about having sex with me. What seemed like a fair trade back at the bar has now become a reality, and she's lost whatever enthusiasm she originally had. It's like when your friend invites you to the opera for the fifth time. You've made shitty excuses four times, hoping she'd get the clue, but she didn't, and you don't want to be rude, so you say, "That sounds lovely!" And it does, since it's four weeks away. But as the date approaches, you start getting angry at yourself for agreeing. You start thinking up excuses, but nothing sounds plausible, and you know your friend's expecting you to bail at the last minute.

What I'm saying, Jackie no longer wants to fuck me. Well, that's not a big deal. I'm used to *that*. She's experiencing regret, and can't think of a good excuse for wasting my time, so she's humiliating me, hoping I'll call off the blow job. Sort of like when your wife hates you and wants a divorce, but doesn't want her friends to think she's the culprit. So she talks badly about you and treats you as shitty as possible, hoping you'll finally demand a divorce. When you can't take it anymore, she'll get what she wants, and be able to convince her friends she's the victim.

In today's world, getting laid by a hot woman half your age requires two things: negotiation and self-loathing. It's what I call the Currency of Copulation, and here's how it works:

Start by putting everything you bring to the table on one side of the equation, and everything she brings on the other. If your side comes up short (and it *will*), you'll need to add the hassle factor you're willing to accept to reach a perfect balance of value. For example, on the left side of the equation, I'm decent looking, well-dressed, freshly-showered, own a five million dollar Manhattan penthouse apartment, and driving a million dollar Porsche. I'm also highly-skilled, incredibly wealthy, and famous around the world in medical circles. On the right side of the equation, she's young and hot.

So my side comes up short.

Which means I have to add in the hassle factor: I bought her a drink, gave her $500 in cash; drove her where she wanted to go, in the car of her dreams.

—And since my side *still* comes up short, I also have to endure her insults, anger, and vomiting threats. In addition, I have to swallow my pride and stand my ground.

With all this on my side of the equation—coupled with the absence of the man she hoped would be here to save her (assuming that was her motive in coming), and the lack of any other viable alternative to pressing her lips to my mighty sword—it seemed the Currency of Copulation had finally balanced. But now she's feeling under-compensated, so I say, "Would it help if I offered you more cash?"

"No."

"What would do the trick?"

"I'd need less self-respect."

"No problem. I can say with certainty you'll have a lot less self-respect the moment we're finished here."

"Obviously. But I need it in advance."

I take a deep breath and assume a matter-of-fact tone: "I understand you're having second thoughts. Sadly, I get that a lot. Perhaps it'll help if I tell you how the other ladies handled it: they owned up to their lack of judgment, accepted our sexual encounter as the low point in their lives, found the inner strength to get through the experience by whatever means necessary, and resolved from that moment forward to elevate their dating standards."

"I bet they were terrible in bed."

"Most were. But bad sex beats no sex."

"Did they request narcotics?"

"Some did."

"That might help."

"Sorry, that option's not available. I've got plans for tonight, and can't babysit you for the next four hours until you're completely lucid."

"Then I'm afraid we've reached an impasse."

"I don't think so. The reality is you made a commitment, accepted money for it, and even bragged how you were going to be the best lay of my life. And if you think I'm going to let it slide just because you're having second thoughts and insulting me, you obviously don't know who you're dealing with. Whatever you say to me...however disgusting I am to you...however horribly you might feel right now or how miserable you might be afterward—has no effect. I just want some pussy or a blow job."

She looks at my penis one last time and says, "I can't believe I agreed to this."

"Me either. But since you did..."

To which she replies, "I'd rather die."

"You don't mean that."

She sets her jaw. "I do." Then she says, "Release me from my promise, or I swear to God I'll jump off the cliff."

I laugh.

"Last chance," she says.

"Sorry."

To my surprise, she pushes the door open, races to the edge of the cliff, and launches herself into space like she's one of those TV cops, jumping from one rooftop to the next. Only there's no rooftop for her to jump to. She seems to freeze in mid-air for half a second, then plummets straight down. I have no idea how far she's falling, but her scream lasts three full seconds before all goes silent.

In situations like these I always try to find the good, and focus on it. Yes, I called her bluff and learned she'd rather die than give me sex; and yes, I'm the last person to see her alive, so instead of being my alibi, the police might consider her my second murder victim of the evening. But the good news is, when they find her body there'll be no evidence of sexual assault, no proof I killed her, and best of all, 911 still has her voice on their recording, not mine. With this information—and Jackie unable to refute my claims—my top-notch attorney should be able to craft a defense sufficient to keep me off death row.

In the meantime, I need to get this car back to the hospital as quickly as possible and act like I've been there the whole time.

I pull my pants up, start the engine, steer Judson's car onto the main road, and think about what Jackie said to me back in the tavern: "If you take me to Inspiration Point I'll give you a memory to last a lifetime."

Well, she did.

Chapter 11

I'M ON A lucky streak. Not only do I make it back to the hospital without incident, I'm able to park Judson's car in the exact space I found it several hours earlier. Now all I have to do is sneak back in the ER and get Judson's keys in his bag undetected. I manage to get all the way to the side entrance of the ER before my luck runs out. As I approach the door, a large man suddenly emerges from the shadows, blocking my way.

Donovan Creed.

"Nice car," he says.

"Thanks. You ever drive one?"

"No."

"You should. It'll change your life."

"I believe you. Should I get the keys from you? Or Judson Bray?"

Creed knows about Bray? Shit! That's bad. Very bad.

I ask, "What brings you here?"

"The favor."

"Right."

I feel his eyes boring in on me. "Anything wrong, Doc?"

"No, of course not. It's just...this isn't the best time to have this discussion."

"There's never a perfect time for what I'm going to say. But I wouldn't be here if it wasn't urgent."

The spot where we're standing would be pitch black if not for the small square window near the top of the door behind him that's casting enough light for him to study my expression as he says: "In two...or possibly three days, a critically ill infant boy will be rushed to your operating room in dire need of emergency surgery."

I nod solemnly and say, "I'll do all I can to save him. You have my word."

"Wrong answer," he says.

"What do you mean?"

"The kid needs to die."

"*What? Why?*"

"That's not your concern. This is the favor I'm calling in."

"And if I refuse?"

"That's not an option."

I laugh. "You're threatening to *kill* me? Fine. Kill me! I'd welcome death with open arms!"

"You say that now. But it won't be a pleasant death."

"Maybe not, but I'd welcome it just the same. I've contemplated suicide many times."

"What stopped you?"

"I have the desire, but not the guts."

"When this is over, if you're still interested, I'd be happy to kill you. For a fee."

"Why the hell would I *pay* you to kill me?"

"It's my job."

"No. I mean, you've already threatened to kill me for *free!*"

"The killing's free. It's the *manner* of killing that's worth whatever I charge. But why do *you* care what it costs? You'll be dead."

"Let's talk about the kid," I say. "If you know anything about me, you know the only thing in this world I care about are the kids they wheel into my operating room. The hopeless cases. The ones every other doctor has given up on."

"I know that. I also know you haven't lost one yet. What's the current streak? Seventy-two?"

I nod.

"That's fine work, Doc, and it's the very reason they'll want to bring this child to *you* in a couple of days."

"I won't kill him."

"I'm not asking you to *kill* him," Creed says. "I'm asking you to let him die."

"This doesn't sound like you, Donovan."

He shrugs. "Desperate times."

"Surely there's another way to achieve whatever goal you're pursuing."

"There is, and we're working on it. But this is our fallback position. If the kid shows up in your operating room, he has to die."

"Donovan? I can't do this. Anything else you need, say the word and it's yours. Or kill me right now, if you like. But I can't allow a child to die on my watch. I...*can't*."

"Take a moment to think how ridiculous that sounds."

"What do you mean?"

"If I kill you tonight you won't be here to save the kid. They'll wheel him into to the *second*-best surgeon's operating room, and he'll certainly die."

"Sounds like a perfect solution to your problem."

"Except that talent like yours needs to exist in the world. Apart from this one child I'd like you to live long enough to save hundreds more. Plus, you and I have a history. I consider you a valuable resource."

"One that you can exploit personally?"

"When necessary."

"Even more reason to ask me for a different favor. Something that doesn't involve the death of an innocent child."

"You've killed patients before."

"Not my *own*!" I say, indignantly.

He laughs.

I quickly add, "You can't prove that."

He says, "I don't have to kill you, Doc. I can make your life a living hell."

"I believe you," I say. Then think about it and add: "Just to be clear, what are we talking about? I mean, do you already have a plan for ruining my life?"

"You know I do."

"Will you tell me?"

"No."

I sigh. "You're asking me to do something that goes against every fiber of my being. If you truly consider me a valuable asset, it's only fair that you at least explain why this child has to die."

He says, "Take ten minutes to check on Judson, and do whatever else you need to do. Then meet me in the hospital cafeteria."

"Thank you."

"Don't be late."

Chapter 12

REMEMBER MY TWO young friends? The PA and medical student who got the hypodermic needle stuck in the patient's backbone a few hours ago? I start by tracking them down and securing their promises to vouch for me. If asked, they'll say I've been here all evening. Next, I review Judson's test results, then enter his room, reminding myself to act as casual as if I'd spent the past three hours watching Hillbilly Hand Fishing instead of stealing his car, breaking into his home, discovering his wife's body, saving her life, contaminating the crime scene, fleeing it, picking up a hooker for an alibi, attempting to seduce her, witnessing her suicide, fleeing the scene of *that* crime, and having my life threatened by a professional hitman.

"How do you feel?" I ask, noting the bag containing his personal items has been moved to a chair within his field of vision.

"Much better," Judson says. "Any word on my test results?"

"So far, so good," I say. "Close your eyes for me, please, and keep them closed."

He does, and I dim the lights and speak loudly to hide the sounds I make while sliding his keys back in his bag: "We've completed the three tests recommended for chest pain under the current emergency room guidelines."

Now, beside him, I say, "Open your eyes, please."

He does, and I remove a penlight from my pocket and ask him to keep his head still while following the light with his eyes as I move it across his field of vision. Testing his eye muscles has nothing to do with his chest pains, but it keeps him from wondering why I had him close his eyes in the first place. As he diligently follows the light it strikes me I could ask him to bark like a dog and he'd do it, since I'm a doctor and he has no idea what I might be measuring. No wonder we doctors are so full of ourselves! It's *your* fault, patients.

Judson asks, "Is everything okay?"

"Is your wife here?"

"No. I called her twice, but she didn't answer. I think she might be stuck in the waiting room. You think someone can check for me?"

"She's not in the waiting room."

"You already checked?"

"No, but if she asked for you they would've escorted her to your bedside." Seeing his phone on his bed I ask, "Want me to call her again?"

He perks up. "That'd be great! Thank you!"

"No problem."

I pick it up, press the button, and listen as it rings six times and goes to voicemail. Then I say, "Mrs. Bray, this is Doctor Box. Your husband has been asking about you, and based on our previous phone conversation I anticipated your arrival by now. That said, if you have any questions about his current condition, or the tests we've run, please feel free to call me at—"

I give her my personal number, end the call, and place his phone back on the bed.

He says, "Can you give me details about my test results?"

My phone vibrates. I check the message. It's Creed, telling me to hurry things along.

I tell Judson: "The EKG measures electrical activity in the heart. Yours was normal. Echocardiogram measures blood flow in the heart, and *that* was normal. Your CT scan also came back normal. I can say with near certainty you didn't have a heart attack."

"So I'm fine?"

"For now, I'd say yes. But if I were you I'd call your cardiologist first thing tomorrow morning, tell him what happened, and see if he wants to schedule additional tests. In the meantime, we'll send him these results."

"Are you saying I'm free to go?"

"I am."

"Earlier you said I'd be here eight hours."

"I assumed we'd find something wrong. We didn't."

"So I'm safe to drive?"

"Yes."

He looks uneasy, so I lower my voice and say, "Remember the blood test I ordered? I took the liberty of screening you for a heart-related biomarker. It's quite effective for ruling out heart attacks based on chest pain. That, plus a normal EKG means your chances of having a heart attack in the next week are roughly 1 in 600."

"Really?"

"I'm not supposed to tell you that, because it's based on a scientific study done in Sweden that hasn't been approved here in the states. But since I'm allowed to get your blood, I figured, why not check the biomarker? So I did, and yours looks good."

"Thanks," he says. "I appreciate that."

"No problem."

Judson doesn't know it, but I also checked his blood for illicit drugs without his consent. Not because I'm nosey, but because one particular drug, cocaine, can cause painful coronary artery spasms, and the go-to medication for heart-attack symptoms is beta-blockers. But beta-blockers can make cocaine-induced spasms life-threatening. Patients never self-report cocaine use, so I—like other decent doctors—often invade your privacy by screening your blood for illegal drugs.

Of course, I also do it to find out if you have other biomarkers I can exploit, or if you have an addiction I can feed or use against you, if you cross me.

My phone buzzes again. This time it's the wife of my arch enemy, Bruce Luce, whose primary goal in life is to destroy me. Bruce is the reason I'm doing five days of ER duty. He's punishing me for my latest transgression (writing humorous code words on a patient's hospital records). Bruce's wife, Truth, hates me even more than *he* does, but I found her weakness, and plan to use her to get to him.

I text her to meet me in 45 minutes, then exit Judson's room and tell the staff to get his discharge paperwork together so he can sign the release forms and get the fuck out of our hospital before someone kills him. Then I head for the cafeteria and hope Creed isn't too pissed at me for being late.

As I enter, I see him sitting in a booth, doing something that seems so totally incongruous I fear I might be losing my mind.

Chapter 13

CREED'S EATING A chocolate-dipped ice cream cone.

I do a double take.

If you told me he walked through the courtyard, reached into the sky, grabbed a pigeon in mid-flight, ripped its head off and ate it for a snack—I'd believe you. But this?

No way.

He notes my expression, shrugs, and points to the sign on the wall advertising our standard hospital cafeteria ice cream cone with "magic" topping. As I slide into the seat opposite him he says, "Dani Ripper helped you with a case once, didn't she?"

"Yeah. By phone. But...she doesn't like me. Why do you ask?"

He holds up what's left of his cone and says, "This is the sort of thing Dani would comment on."

I humor him: "What would Dani say?"

He smiles. "I can't imitate her voice, but I expect she'd say, 'Magic? *Seriously?* It's melted chocolate that turns into a hard shell when it touches something cold. I'm not saying it isn't fun, or that it's tasteless, but it's hardly magic. Magic would be if the ice cream changes colors, grows tits, and starts dancing the merengue!'"

He laughs.

I'm not clever, or funny, or whatever he thinks Dani Ripper is, but since I value my life and the lives of my patients, I decide to show him that Dani's not the only one who can recognize hyperbole. I say, "You know who Big Bird is?"

He gives me an odd look. "You mean the Sesame Street character that looks like Howard Stern?"

I nod.

"What about him?"

"The guy who plays him has been doing it for 45 years."

"So?"

"They made a movie about him, a documentary, and called him a genius. Not just once, but repeatedly. Now I'm sure he's a loving, caring guy with a childlike spirit, but if he's a *genius*, what the hell does that make *me*? I mean, no offense, but while this guy's zipping on his fucking *bird* suit I'm bringing dead kids back to life on an operating table!"

Creed stares at me a moment before saying, "Can you make the voice?"

"What voice?"

"Big Bird."

"No."

"I see. But would you be willing to put on a bird suit every day of your life for 45 years to entertain children and bring joy to their lives?"

"Of course not."

He shows me a smug smile, and if I had any sense I'd shut the fuck up and pretend he made some sort of point. Unfortunately, when it comes to keeping my mouth shut, I'm like a Toon when exposed to the *Shave and a Haircut* knock. I *have* to respond! So I say, "Perhaps I should retire and let Big Bird operate on hopeless case infants from now on."

Before I can say "Just kidding!" Creed says, "I spent two hours reviewing your psychiatric profile this morning, and...it's quite disturbing."

"I have no idea what you've been studying, but it wasn't *my* profile," I say. "I've never been to a psychiatrist in my entire life."

"It was your profile, all right. I personally commissioned it."

"In other words, it's based on conjecture."

"It's based on everything you've done in your life when you thought no one was looking."

"Who put it together?"

"My geeks."

"Are you referring to the midgets that work at your headquarters in Virginia?"

"*One* midget," he says. "The others are a dwarf, and an elf."

"Elf?"

"We're getting off point."

"I agree. So why do you want me to let this kid die?"

"National security."

"How can an infant possibly affect the security of the United States?"

"It's a long story," he says, "and you were late getting here, so I'll give you the short version. The one without footnotes and theological explanations."

"What type of theology condones killing children?"

He holds up a hand to quiet me, but ice cream is dripping from it. Creed frowns at his cone, as if it's the ice cream's fault his fingers are sticky. He clearly doesn't care for his treat, but doesn't seem to know what to do with it, so he watches it leak from his hand a moment before finally placing it on the table. Now his fingers are full of melted ice cream and chocolate, and it's annoying the shit out of him to the point he's lost the thread of his own conversation.

I may not be genius enough to dress in a bird costume and talk with a funny voice, but as a trained surgeon who's used to making split-second life and death decisions, I put that training to use, saying "I'll get you a napkin!"

I rush to the counter, get some napkins, stop at the soda fountain, wet some of them, bring them back to the table, attempt to hand them to Creed, but notice he's already licking his fingers. I frown, use the napkins to wipe the mess from the tabletop, then wrap the remnants of his ice cream cone in them and take the whole nasty mess to the trash can.

...And suddenly realize he manipulated me into cleaning up his mess! Without saying a word, he used some sort of neuro-linguistic programming to create an imprint on my mind that subconsciously made me want to do his bidding.

There's no doubt I'm vastly superior to this guy intellectually, but he's obviously some sort of mind-control expert, or master manipulator, so I caution myself not to underestimate him.

When I return to the table he says, "I assume you're familiar with Wall Street?"

"Are you referring to the stock market?"

"No. I'm talking about the actual street that runs seven-tenths of a mile from Broadway to South in the Financial District of Lower Manhattan. It cuts through eight city blocks"

"What about it?"

"A terrorist named Yasin Salib intends to blow up one of the blocks."

"When?"

"Soon."

"Which block?"

"We don't know yet."

"How would killing the infant solve the problem?"

Creed scans the room, then lowers his voice and says, "It's Salib's son."

He pauses a moment, then adds: "Salib belongs to a religious sect that believes the only way a man's lineage can survive is if his firstborn son enters Paradise. And that can only happen if Salib dies first to pave the way, or if he prays over his son's dead body for 12 hours prior to burial, which is required to take place within three days."

I shake my head. "Atheism is so much simpler."

"How so?"

"This endless terrorism you fight every day: how much is justified by religious beliefs?"

"A hundred percent."

"And isn't it true that more wars have been fought in the name of religion than all other causes combined?"

"What's your point?"

I shrug. "Personally, I don't care what others believe. If the President of the United States believes in Santa Claus, more power to him. But if he starts passing laws based on Santa's teachings, I've got a major problem."

"I'll pass that along next time I see him."

"The President?"

"No. Santa. Meanwhile, here's the situation: we have credible intelligence Salib and his terror cell plan to blow an entire city block off the map."

"I still don't see the connection to his child."

"Salib and his people will have to sacrifice their lives to pull this off. I've got a dozen people working the area, but the chances of uncovering the explosives are minimal, since they probably haven't been placed yet. And even if they have, there's no way twelve people can properly search eight blocks of Lower Manhattan."

"Get more searchers."

"More searchers would tip off Salib and his people. If he gets wind we're onto him, he'll change the target."

"Why not evacuate the buildings on those days?"

He shakes his head. "I don't expect you to understand how terrorism works."

"Try me."

"If we evacuate Wall Street for two days they'll simply delay the attack or change the target. But imagine what they will have accomplished: they will have shut down New York's Financial District, which would be a *huge* victory for them. Not only would it be front-page news around the world, it would also encourage more recruits to join their movement, which elevates the terrorist threat exponentially. It's simply not an option."

"So if I'm following you correctly, Salib plans to sacrifice his life while committing a legendary act of terrorism, believing his death will pre-date his son's."

"Exactly."

"How ill is his son?"

"He's not ill at all. He's perfectly healthy."

"Then...I mean, how—"

Chapter 14

"I HAVE SOMEONE on the inside," Creed says. "Someone close to the child, who has the means to make him sick enough to get him to the hospital. Sick enough to require emergency surgery."

"Why not just have your person kill the kid?"

"He won't do it."

"Why not?"

Creed shrugs. "It's against his religion."

"How is it not against his religion to make the kid sick enough to die?"

"I've assured my contact if the mother brings him to your hospital, you'll save his life."

"And yet you're ordering me to kill him."

"Again, you don't have to *kill* him, you just can't *save* him."

I don't expect a guy like Creed to understand not saving the kid is the same as killing him, but I'd like to suggest a very simple alternate plan: "Correct me if I'm wrong, but if you're trying to prevent the Wall Street attack, the kid doesn't have to die. You could have your contact make the kid sick enough for surgery, rush him to the hospital, and while I'm saving his life, your people can capture Salib."

"Two problems," he says. "First, Salib's the mastermind, but he's only one part of the terror cell. If we get him the others are free to complete the attack without him. And second, I can't capture him if I don't know where he is."

"I assume he'll come to the hospital to check on his son."

"That would never happen. Salib will remain hidden and wait to hear about his son's condition. When he learns his son has died he'll insist the body be brought to him at a safe location so he can pray over it."

"The hospital's not going to just hand over the body of an infant who died under suspicious circumstances. What about all the red tape?"

"That's where *you* come in. You'll personally issue the medical certificate showing cause of death, and give valid reasons why a coroner's post-mortem examination isn't necessary. You'll explain why his immediate release is necessary to accommodate Salib's religious beliefs. Then you'll make sure the body goes directly to the hospital morgue until the family arranges to collect it."

I close my eyes, shake my head. This is insane. But it's a well-known fact that Creed's highly connected, so if anyone can pull it off, he's the guy. Still, if the kid dies I'll definitely want to attend his funeral, which I could only do if a funeral home's involved. So I ask, "After the prayer ceremony, do you think the family will have a public or private service?"

Creed looks at me like I've lost my mind. "If we do our job right there won't *be* any family left to host a funeral."

"You're planning to kill the whole family?"

"If possible."

"How?"

"From the moment of death, Salib has just 60 hours to start praying, in order to get the 12-hours completed prior to the burial. And the praying has to take place beside the body."

I see where this is going: "When the people pick the kid up from the hospital morgue you'll follow them to the safe house. When you're sure Salib, his family, and the terrorists are all in the same place at the same time, you'll attack."

"Salib's far too cautious for that. He'll have people stationed everywhere, keeping an eye out for any suspicious activity. They won't take the child's body directly to the safe house. They'll go through areas where my people and I would stand out like sore thumbs. If they have the slightest indication they're being followed they'll never take the kid to Salib. If that happens, the kid will have died for nothing."

I'm hopelessly confused. "If you can't follow the family, how do you plan to find and kill Salib?"

He pauses before saying, "The answer to that question goes to the very heart of why I need you in the operating room, owing me a favor."

I suddenly get it: "I know what you're going to say."

He looks surprised. "You do? Let's hear it."

"You want me to implant a tracking device in the kid's body."

He smiles. "Close, but no cigar. Here's the plan: after the kid dies and the nurses clear the room, you're going to implant an explosive device into his corpse. Later on, when Salib leans over the body to pray for his son's entry into Paradise, I'll detonate it and blow the motherfucker to hell, along with all his friends, family, and terror associates."

My jaw drops. "You can't be serious."

"Guess again."

"You're insane."

"Coming from you, that's quite a pronouncement."

"Obviously I'm going to refuse."

His expression turns curious. "What do you mean *obviously?*"

"There's no way I'll be able to implant a bomb in a dead kid's body! It's impossible."

"Why not? After calling time of death you'll order your nurses out of the room, implant the device into one of the wounds you've made, then sew it up."

"What about the video?"

"What video?"

"All surgeries in our hospital are filmed in vivid, graphic detail."

"Since when?"

"Since medical malpractice became our biggest expense."

"I'll get my people on it."

"What's that supposed to mean?"

"It means you do your job, I'll do mine. I'll find a way to disable the cameras at the appropriate time. Trust me."

I look at him. "And if I refuse to participate?"

"If you don't do this for me, I'll have zero use for you."

"Except that you said earlier you considered me a useful asset for the future."

"That's my preference, but I won't compromise this mission." He looks at his watch. "I'll give you five minutes to decide."

"Why five minutes?"

"Remember when you fetched the napkins for my ice cream cone a few minutes ago?"

How could I not? The whole incident was absurd. I'm practically smiling even now, just thinking about it: big, tough Donovan Creed rendered helpless by an ice cream cone!

"Yeah, I remember," I say. "What about it?"

"Look at your hands."

I do. Shockingly, they're a frightening shade of crimson. As are my wrists.

He says, "The napkins you handled were laced with a contact poison that requires an antidote be administered within 15 minutes if death is to be avoided."

As I stare at him in horror, he removes a hypodermic needle from his pocket and says, "Are you with me or against me?"

I'm absolutely stunned. Again I find myself totally out-maneuvered by a guy who possesses half my intellect. For the second time I make a silent vow to never underestimate him again. Of *course* I want the antidote! But there's something I absolutely have to know.

"Can I ask you one question?"

"Of course. But you'd better make it quick."

Chapter 15

MY QUESTION TO Creed: "If you prevent this attack, how many people are likely to be saved?"

"Between ten and twenty thousand."

"What makes *their* lives so special?"

He looks at me like I'm on *Naked and Afraid*, and the one survival item I brought was a door knob. Then says, "I don't understand the question."

"There are too many people in the world already," I say. "Why are those ten to twenty thousand more important than Salib's son?"

"If Salib's attack is successful, he'll be a martyr. Tens of thousands will join their cause, and his son will probably grow up to become a famous terrorist, and the cycle will continue."

"Yeah, but next week or next month you'll have a totally *different* terrorist threat, just as dangerous."

"Almost certainly. And I'll deal with that one when it comes."

"When will it stop?"

He shrugs. "When will they stop bringing dying infants to your operating room?"

"Never."

"Same answer."

I look at my arms. They're red to my elbows. "Okay. Give me the antidote."

Creed cocks his head. "Are you saying—"

"Yeah."

"I'd feel better if you say it out loud."

"If they bring the kid to my operating room, I'll make sure he dies."

"And?"

"I'll implant the bomb."

"You swear?"

I nod.

He puts the syringe back in his pocket, gets to his feet.

"*Creed!*" I say, hearing the panic in my voice. "I said I'll do it!"

"I heard you."

"Then...give me the antidote!"

He reaches back into his pocket, hands me two pills.

I stare at them. "*Benadryl?*"

He shrugs again. "I may have exaggerated the danger of the substance I placed on the napkins."

"You were *bluffing* me?"

"Not at all. If you had refused to help me, you still would have begged me to give you the syringe, correct?"

I nod.

"And I would have gladly done so, because *that's* where the deadly poison resides."

He gives me a few seconds to consider how, just seconds ago, I would have eagerly injected myself with a deadly poison, thinking it would save my life. Then he pats my shoulder and says, "I'll be in touch."

Chapter 16

I SWALLOW THE Benadryl, but remain seated a few minutes while plotting my next move. And I *need* one, since I have no intention of letting Salib's baby die. Not only that, but did you catch that part of the conversation where he thinks I'd actually consider implanting a *bomb* in a dead child's chest?

Only Creed could think to blow up a grieving father while he's praying over his dead son, and use the dead son's body as the murder weapon! How can this possibly be the only solution to locating Salib and ending his bomb threat?

Creed is so crazy and unstable I marvel at his ability to function without constant supervision from a team of highly-trained medical personnel.

I need a plan.

One that Creed would never suspect.

It shouldn't be too difficult. Despite what's happened, I'm not ready to concede that Creed's intellect is any higher than your typical NFL commissioner's. That said, he *has* forced me to admit he's craftier than I would have expected. With each encounter, he's teaching me more and more about how he thinks, and that's a mistake on his part. I'm pretty good at pegging a person's IQ, and I'd put Creed's somewhere below the genius range of 140 to 159.

By contrast, mine is 180, which puts me in the rarified category of *super genius*.

I know what you're thinking: I begged him for the antidote, and he tricked me into thinking the syringe held the antidote and not the poison. But that doesn't make him smarter than I am, or even close. He simply had a plan, and I didn't, which means he caught me by surprise. But now that I know what he wants and when he wants it, the power shifts to me.

I meant what I said earlier: I'm not afraid to die, and might actually welcome death, because—let's face it—it sucks being me. Yeah, I'm impossibly brilliant, wealthy, and live a great lifestyle, but I have serious antisocial tendencies, an overdeveloped sense of revenge, no friends, and fully despise the one thing I'm good at: my job.

I dislike people.

That can't surprise you, knowing I haven't given Jackie Fish's death a second thought. Jackie, the sad soul who came into my life, offering warmth and companionship, then killed herself a little more than an hour ago.

Have I made my point? Let's put it this way: smart and successful as I am, Tom Brady isn't likely to swap lives with me anytime soon. So it's to my advantage that Creed thinks I value my life more than I do.

I shake my head thinking about it. Had I entered the cafeteria with the vaguest notion he might try to kill me I probably would have resigned myself to dying. But it never dawned on me he'd consider killing me in the hospital cafeteria in front of a dozen witnesses. Or to be more precise, that he'd trick me into killing myself.

This, after announcing he considered me a valuable asset to his future!

How strange would it have been to be found dead in the booth of a hospital cafeteria, with a syringe beside me!

Like I said, he caught me by surprise, and that's the genius of Creed. He might not be a genius in *fact*, but he certainly operates at a genius level when it comes to scheming and plotting and understanding human tendencies. He's a magician. A master at creating mental and physical diversions, and by the way...

He manipulated me like a ventriloquist manipulates a dummy. Like the media manipulates the masses. Like...

I smile.

I just figured out how to handle this thing with Creed.

Will it work?

It *has* to.

Because if you go after the king, you'd better kill him. Hypothetically, at least.

I leave the cafeteria with renewed confidence, step into the hallway restroom to pee, and notice the fancy new jet air dryer mounted on the wall where the paper towel dispenser used to be.

Idiots!

Want to know what's going on here? Some medical supply salesman convinced the hospital bean counters this machine would save money and trees over time, and no one bothered to consult a health expert about the risks. I get it: aside from the possible ear damage caused by the horrific noise, it just *seems* plausible that jet air dryers create a more sterile environment. But the truth is these germ blowers disperse 27 *times* more microbes into the air than paper towels! A typical blast sends airborne bacteria swirling throughout the bathroom for up to 15 minutes! In a *hospital*, for God's sake!

I suppose our board of directors will sleep better at night knowing Shit Fuck Hospital is working very diligently to spread MRSA in the most cost-effective manner possible. Now all we need to do is...

Hang on a sec. My phone's ringing.

I listen for a moment, then say, "Your timing's perfect. I'm on my way."

Chapter 17

AS YOU KNOW, Bruce Luce, our hospital administrator, hates me.

Hates me so much he can't even bring himself to acknowledge my ability as a surgeon. Hates me so much he'd fire me every day of his life if he could...

But he can't afford to.

Credit where credit's due: Bruce is one of the world's best fundraisers, and he's the reason Shit Fuck hospital is still in business. How good is he? He's raised a whopping $212 million in donations over the past three years!

Unfortunately for Bruce, every dollar of that was generated through the power of my name. Despite what he thinks of me personally, in the eyes of the hospital's benefactors, I'm a rock star. My name, medical reputation, and results provide them with hours of country club conversation each month, and fill their greedy little hearts with pride. Which means Bruce's continuing employment is predicated on keeping me out of trouble with the Board.

But lately his actions suggest he must have a career death wish, since he's been petitioning the Board to have me fired. He stays up at night studying the resumes of up-and-coming surgeons he dreams might replace me someday, and makes my job as difficult as possible by undermining me with the nurses and forcing me to work exclusively with hopeless-case patients. If I manage to lose a few—or even one!—he feels he can make a case to the Board that I'm expendable.

Are you getting this? If you want to know how ugly office politics can get, look no further than Bruce Luce, for here we have a hospital administrator who secretly hopes at least a few of the patients he sends me will die under my care!

That's raw, unadulterated hate. But you know who hates me even worse?

His wife, Truth.

Which is why you'll be surprised to learn she's my date tonight!

No need to raise your eyebrows over this news, since Truth would sooner strangle a puppy with her bare hands than classify our upcoming meeting as a date. But since I plan to see her naked, and perhaps even molest her—with her permission, of course (her *general* permission)—it certainly satisfies *my* definition of a date!

Helpful background information as to how this is possible: Truth is addicted to pain killers. Heavily addicted. I'd go so far as to say *hopelessly* addicted.

She's gone the full monty to overcome it: intervention, medication, counseling, therapy...she even completed a four-week stint in a fashionable detox facility.

To no avail.

It's not surprising: opioid addiction is one of the worst known to man. It alters your brain. And the more susceptible you are to its influence, the harder it is to break the cycle of dependency. Truth is more dependent on pain killers than anyone I've ever known. It's put her marriage, friendships, social life, and personal health at serious risk. She's not to the point where she'd murder her children to get a fix...but she might consider it for a lifetime scrip.

Well, that's unreasonably harsh. I doubt she'd murder her children for any reason. But my point is Truth craves drugs like Caitlyn Jenner craves taffeta.

With his job and reputation on the line, Bruce was forced to terminate Truth's access to all forms of pain medication. Now *she's* miserable, *he's* miserable, and they're barely speaking to each other. From his perspective, the hospital administrator's wife has a class 5 addiction. From her perspective, her husband—the hospital administrator—has access to the one thing in life she wants: drugs. Jeez, people! We've got a marriage at stake! Won't someone step forward and solve these kids' problems?

Cue the hero!

Last week I snuck up on Truth at a fundraiser Bruce scheduled in my honor. Before she could duck away or secretly spit on me, I offered an intriguing proposition. I whispered in her ear: "We don't like each other, but I have a solution for your chronic pain. Call me."

"I'd rather die," she said, which, as you know by now, is a phrase I frequently hear from women of all ages, shapes, and sizes.

But she did, in fact, call the next morning to ask what I meant. And I said, "I know you've been suffering, and I can help."

"You'll prescribe pills?" she said.

"Even better."

"What could be better?"

"I'd rather not say over the phone. Let's meet."

"Publicly, of course."

"Of course."

We met at a Starbucks, and I told her Bruce was trying to come up with a way of punishing me that wouldn't hurt his fundraising efforts, but would make me completely miserable.

She said, "Is this about the notes you wrote on a patient's chart?"

I nodded. "A nurse ratted me out. How much do you know about it?"

"Just that you wrote something inappropriate on a dying child's chart and he went to the Board to have you fired. They refused, and told him to punish you instead. But Bruce said every time he tries to punish you, you threaten to quit. And the hospital can't afford for you to quit."

She paused a moment, then asked, "What did you write on the chart?"

"*Patient's mother suffers from CTT. Possible SFT user.*"

"What does that mean?"

"CTT is Chronic Twinkie Toxicity. My way of saying she's a fat fuck."

Truth frowned so deeply her wrinkles could have hidden a sandwich. She took a deep breath. "What's SFT?"

"It means she possibly uses sheep for tampons."

The expression of contempt Truth gave me would've made a bystander think I'd confessed to sodomizing a squirrel.

"It was just some random chart-writing," I said.

She rolled her eyes. "It was a horrible mistake."

"Not a mistake," I said. "A joke."

She shakes her head. "Not the chart, you idiot. Coming here. Meeting you. Occupying the same general space. Taking a chance on being seen in public with you."

She got up to leave, but I stopped her with: "In the space of one hour I can make you pain free for three days."

She sat back down. "You said you wouldn't give me pills."

"I didn't say I *wouldn't*. I said I can offer you something better."

"Like what?"

"A massage technique."

Her face blanched. "Fuck you!"

"I'm serious, Truth. Give it a try. If it's not better than pills, I'll give you all the pills you want."

"You're trying to set me up."

I handed her a small plastic bottle. "This is Oxycodone, 15 milligrams," I said. "Twelve tabs should get you through...how long?"

"Two days, max."

"Fine. Take them. When you're ready for something stronger, give me a call."

She looked around the coffee shop before accepting them. "What type of massage are you talking about?"

"Fentanyl."

Her eyes went as wide as eyes can go, and the reason was—as every pain junkie knows—no medication on earth is stronger than fentanyl, a drug so powerful and addictive the DEA tracks every prescription. Fentanyl is the final drug given to chronic pain patients at the last stage of their lives.

"How strong is it, really?" she asked.

"It's morphine times 100."

"That can't be true."

"Look it up."

"How does it compare to heroin?"

"Fentanyl's 20 times more potent than heroin."

She paused a moment to contemplate that statement. Then said, "Is it safe?"

"Are you serious? *Hell* no! Which is why you need me."

"I know it's hard to come by, but if you could see your way to acquire a few fentanyl patches, I might be able to—"

I waved her off. "Too dangerous. Even those with the highest tolerance are certain to overdose. And—nothing personal, but you don't have the knowledge or experience to properly dilute it. Almost no one does. It's a fiercely dangerous drug that requires special formulation. After months of testing, I've perfected it, along with a unique delivery method."

"Massage," she said, frowning.

"That's right."

"And I'm supposed to trust *you?*"

"You could do worse. I've never lost a patient."

"This sounds completely shady."

"Shadier than supplying you with narcotics I've stolen from your husband's hospital?"

She thought about it a long time, but not *that* long. Then said, "Don't expect me to remove my clothes."

"It shouldn't come to that," I lied.

"Let me be perfectly clear, Gideon: I will *not* allow you to see me naked."

"Let's not make this a bigger deal than it is."

"What do you mean?"

"We're talking about a solution to your chronic pain. A *solution*, Truth."

We both went quiet till I said, "I'm sure we can adjust your clothing to the extent you feel appropriate for the treatment."

"Now you sound like a lawyer."

"Then let's be specific: you'd have to bare the area of your lower back where the pain is localized."

She frowned. "I'll think about it."

"Wow, *thanks*," I said, sarcastically. "I'm risking the loss of my career and a *prison* sentence for you, and you'll *think* about showing me the few inches of your back necessary to *help* you? *Super!*"

"Oh, shut up!" she said. "I'm just setting some parameters. I won't commit to anything until I hear what you expect in return."

"I want you to suggest something to Bruce."

"What?"

"A way he can punish me."

"Like what?"

"Tell him to make me work in the emergency room for two weeks."

"You'd do that?"

"No, but I'd negotiate him down to five days."

"Why the ER?"

"It's my briar patch."

She stared at me, waiting for an explanation, so I said, "Brer Rabbit begged his arch enemy, Brer Fox, not to throw him in the briar patch. Said he was terrified of the briar patch. So naturally Brer Fox tossed him in the briar patch, and Brer Rabbit had a big laugh because he was *born* in a briar patch. In other words, Bruce will be sending me to the one place I want to go."

"Let me guess: fresh crop of nurses?"

"And?"

"Access to illicit drugs?"

"That would certainly be to *your* benefit."

"Tell me again why I should trust you?"

"Because we can help each other. I'll make you pain free, and you'll feed me inside information about the Board, and Bruce's ongoing plans to fire me."

"That's it?"

"Yes. For now, at least."

"What do you mean?"

"At some point I might need a serious favor, like getting you to vouch for me, or provide an alibi, or testify on my behalf as a character witness. I mean, I don't have anything concrete. I'm basically saying we'd have each other's backs, and in your case I'll *literally* have your back. I'll take care of you, and you'll help protect me. Not because you give a shit about me, but because as long as I've got a job, I have access to what you need."

"I won't break the law."

"Of course you will," I said, pointing to the pill bottle. "You're breaking it right now."

Chapter 18

HERE'S THE SETUP, in real time: I'm standing at the base of the thousand-dollar massage table I've placed in the living room of my penthouse apartment, and Truth Luce is lying facedown on it. She's wearing yoga clothes to reinforce her excuse for being out this late at night: the alleged grand opening of a new fitness studio.

I know she's in severe pain, since it took her more a half-minute to ease herself onto the table. The effort brought tears to her eyes and made her gasp several times. It was pitiful to watch, though I have zero compassion for her.

"You can raise my top," she says, "but only up to my bra strap."

Right. Lucky me.

I lift her top the eight inches I'm allowed, then say, "Can you reach back and touch the spot that hurts the worst?"

"No," she says. "But it's dead center."

I study her back. "Not true."

"I ought to know where I hurt," she says, indignantly.

"I agree. But you're not telling me."

She sighs. "L4, L5, and..."

"Sacrum?"

She says, "I insist you leave my sacrum covered."

"Let's try to remember I'm a doctor."

"Let's try to remember you're a scheming, manipulative, highly unprofessional doctor with serious social and psychological disorders."

"Fair enough. Did you happen to finish swallowing the powder I gave you?"

"Yes. It was vile. If something happens to me, I'll make sure you're punished to the full extent of the law."

"I understand."

I lower her yoga pants three inches, causing her to say, "What the hell are you *doing*?"

"Uncovering the L4 and L5. Nothing more."

I begin probing the area with my fingertips, causing her back to spasm. "*Stop it!*" she shouts every time I do it, which admittedly is several more times than necessary, since I *want* her to hurt like hell. Not because I hate her, but because I want her to fully appreciate the difference the drugs are going to make.

"You were wise not to let them operate," I say.

"How bad is it?"

"As bad as it gets. I don't know how you manage to get through the day."

"If only you could tell my husband. Bruce is convinced it's all in my head."

"Bruce is an asshole."

"Don't try to win me over, Gideon. It won't work. He's twice the man you are."

"I agree. I couldn't possibly run a hospital. But that doesn't mean he understands what you're going through."

"Why is that, do you suppose?"

"He's not a doctor."

"He's seen my x-rays."

"Back pain is hard to quantify with x-rays," I say.

"When is this alleged massage supposed to take place?"

"Almost instantly. Can you raise your right arm and give me a thumbs-up signal?"

She tries, but can't.

"Very well. Here's what I want you to do. Keep your face down at all times. Don't try to turn your head or raise up. I'm not going to lower your pants any further, but I *am* going to perform acupuncture through your clothing at several key spots. You'll feel a small pinch as the needles go in, and—"

"I've had acupuncture several times, Gideon, from different specialists. It didn't work."

"This is different. I wouldn't have even mentioned it, except that I knew you'd feel a prick."

"Are we talking about the needles or *you?*"

"Funny."

"*Ouch!*" she says, feeling the first needle. "*Shit!*" she says, feeling the second. "Have you ever *done* this before?"

"Of course."

"Well, you suck at it! That hurt like *hell!*"

"These needles are different than the crap those idiots used on you."

"I'll have you know those 'idiots' are considered the best acupuncturists in Manhattan. In *their* hands, I barely felt the needles. Compared to what *you* did to me just now—"

I interrupt her: "You can't compare my treatment to theirs, because you already admitted they didn't help you."

"Neither have *you!*"

"Oh no?"

She thinks about it a moment. "Uh...well, I suppose I *do* feel...a little better."

No *shit* she's feeling better! The two shots of morphine I gave her under the guise of acupuncture have effectively deadened her entire ass!

"Try to lift your right arm and give me a thumbs-up."

She makes a second attempt, and although it's close, she's not quite there. I inject her lower back a single time, left side.

"*Shit!*" she yelps.

I wait a few seconds and ask again to give me a thumbs-up.

This time it works.

"That's *amazing!*" she says.

I walk around to the head of the table, place her phone and earbuds in her left hand and say, "In a moment I want you to insert your earbuds and listen to your music. Once you've started, don't stop. But whenever I press my finger into your right foot I want you to lift your right arm as high as possible, and give me a thumbs-up."

"Why?"

"Your range of motion will tell me exactly where to concentrate my efforts."

"Are you planning to rub fentanyl onto my skin?"

"Yes. In a diluted form."

"Will it be like wearing a patch?"

"Yes, but better."

"How so?"

"You'd have to wear a fentanyl patch for three days to get the same relief I'm going to give you during the next hour. I doubt you'd be able to hide the patch from Bruce every day for the rest of your life. This way you'll get the benefit of fentanyl every three days without having to wear the patch."

"*Whoa!*"

"What now?"

"Surely you don't expect me to come here every three *days?*"

"Of course not. But I think you'll *want* to."

"What if I decide I'd rather have Percocet?"

"I hope you *do!* That'd be a helluva lot easier for *me!* I'll give you all the Perc I can, but keep in mind you'll have to hide them from Bruce. And you know he's going to constantly search for your stash."

"Why?"

"Because he's going to be suspicious as to why you've suddenly become pain free. Keep coming here and you won't have to hide anything."

"Except the hourly visit every three days."

"Tell him you like the exercise class."

"I don't think it registered with him tonight. I mean, how the hell could I do a yoga class if I'm in chronic pain?"

"Like I said, Bruce is an asshole."

"He's just distracted. He works hard."

"Whatever."

"How about both?" she says.

"What do you mean?"

"Percocet *and* massage? I'm only asking because it's not practical for me to come here twice a week every single week. But if this works better than Percocet, I'd like to come whenever I can, if you're available. And when I can't come, I'd have the Perc."

"That'll work. Go ahead and put your earbuds in and turn on the music."

After she does, I walk to the side of the table and pull her pants and underwear down to her knees, slap her ass a couple of times knowing she can't feel a thing, then pinch the bottom of her foot, and laugh out loud when she gives me an enthusiastic thumbs-up.

I start massaging the diluted fentanyl into her lower back and upper ass, and then open the bag I placed on a chair earlier, and remove some markers and a small flag. I place the markers in my pocket, and insert the flag—which says, *Property of Gideon Box!*—into Truth's ass. Then I open my cell phone and take a video of her bare ass, including the flag, and say, "Truth, do you *really* love me?" I press her foot and she gives the camera a thumbs-up. Then I say, "What did you think about the anal sex I gave you tonight?" Again I press her foot and she gives me a thumbs-up. Then I put the phone down, write some graffiti on her ass with the markers:

classy stuff like, *Fuck You, Bruce!* And, *Property of Gideon Box*, and so forth. Then I record my handiwork, remove the flag, wipe off the writing; tongue her ass a couple times just to say I did...then get back to the massage.

Truth has been a thorn in my side for years, but I don't want her to suffer. Everything I said to her was completely true: what I could do for her, how it would work, how I'd give her a steady supply of pain pills if she wants them...everything. All true. Except for the acupuncture. As for the video evidence of molestation, I only plan to use it in the event Truth decides to turn on me, set me up, blackmail me, allows Bruce to fire me, or if she causes me some other sort of annoyance.

I suddenly think of a couple more questions to ask, so I get my phone out again and press the record button: "Truth, how big is Bruce's dick?"

I press her foot and she shows me her thumb.

I wait till she puts her arm down, then ask, "Can I put a video of your bare ass on the Internet for the entire world to see?"

I press her foot and get her thumbs-up.

"Thanks, Truth! You're the best!"

I pull her panties and pants back up, then massage her lower back till the sedatives wear off. Then help her to a sitting position and enjoy the wondrous smile she bestows on me for making her feel as euphoric as you'd expect from a drug that's 20 times more powerful than heroin.

Ladies and gentlemen, Truth Luce entered my home generally attractive in that too-thin, middle-aged, wealthy, Manhattan ladies-who-lunch sort of way, except that her body was slumped with pain, and her profile resembled a question mark. Now, after being exposed to Dr. Box's miracle healing treatment for a single hour, she looks 10 years younger as she jumps to her feet and moves about the room athletically, her carriage erect, with a profile that resembles an exclamation point.

"It's a *miracle!*" she gushes.

What was it she said at Starbucks just days ago? She didn't want me to touch her? Refused to let me see her naked?

Ha!

By this time next week she'll refuse me nothing. If I say jump, she'll ask how high. When I tell her to sit, she won't look for a chair.

Please don't misinterpret: I don't want to turn Truth Luce into a worse addict than she already is, and I don't particularly want to fuck her. But I'm willing to do both, to get back at Bruce.

As for Truth, it's obviously a joy to be pain-free, as she can't stop grinning. "I can't believe how incredible I feel! Thank you Gideon."

"Does this mean we're friends?"

She gives me a look that says all the shit that's passed between us over the years has been forgiven and forgotten. "I'd like that, Gideon."

"Me too," I say, flashing my best Sunday smile, marveling how dramatically a relationship can change in the space of an hour through drug therapy.

She leaves my penthouse on such a high she actually forgot to ask for the pain pills. Which means she's planning to come back in three days.

I close the door behind her and smile. Two more sessions like this and I'll own this stuffy, insufferable bitch, body and soul.

She'll be my little meat muppet.

My slut puppy.

My phone vibrates to tell me I've received a text message from Donovan Creed. The message says: *Turn Around.*

Before I can type a response, I get another text: *Turn Around!*

It dawns on me he actually wants me to turn around here in the foyer of my own home. I do, and nearly faint when I see Donovan Creed standing beside the massage table.

He says, "What do *you* think?"

It takes several seconds to regain my composure enough to say, "About what?"

Creed says, "Personally, I thought Truth had a surprisingly nice ass." He aims his phone at me to show he took a video of me as I videoed the flag in her ass. Then he says, "Bruce is gonna shit when he sees this!"

Now that it's clear he's not planning to kill me, I find the courage to be furious: "This building has the top security in the entire city!"

"I agree. But how's that relevant to Truth's ass?"

"There's no way our doorman or security guards would let you enter the lobby without my express permission."

"So?"

Boxed In!

"So how the fuck did you get in here?

Creed shrugs. "I used the back entrance."

"I don't *have* a back entrance."

He smiles. "Yes you do."

Chapter 19

CREED LEADS ME past my kitchen, to the laundry room. I look around before saying, "There's no entrance here."

"Pull your washing machine toward you."

"Why?"

"It's been modified."

He gestures at the washer, so I humor him by gently tugging on it, and to my surprise, it slides three feet toward the center of the room with silent ease. I lean over the washer, look behind it, and see a small wooden panel attached to the wall about two feet high by three feet wide.

"It pops out," Creed says.

I notice metal floor tracks leading from the wall to the current position of the washer, tracks I'd never seen before. I push the machine back against the wall and get on my hands and knees to see why the tracks aren't visible when the washing machine is flush against the wall.

"They retract," Creed says.

I get to my feet and stare at him. "How long has this entrance been here?"

"How long have I known you?"

I take a moment to do the math. "You've been breaking into my home for three *years*?"

"Not constantly. Just when I'm in town and you're at work."

"How do you know when I'm at work?"

"I'm Donovan Creed."

I set my jaw. "Well, it ends today. By this time tomorrow, it'll be bricked up, along with whatever passage it leads to."

"You might want to rethink that."

"Why?"

"It gives you egress."

"Why would I want to crawl out of my penthouse through a hidden door?"

"To avoid the police."

I frown. "Are you threatening me?"

"Of course."

"Why would the police be interested in me?"

"Seriously? How about a lifetime of murders, break-ins, and thefts? More recently you stole a patient's car, drove to his house, went through his things, patched up his dying wife but left her lying on the bathroom floor to die, after tampering with the crime scene."

"How do you *know* that?"

"I keep up with things. Shall I continue? You didn't report the crime, you fled the scene, you failed to call an ambulance."

"Not true."

"Which?"

"I called 911 to report an emergency."

"No you didn't."

"Well...okay, that's true. If we're being technical. But I absolutely arranged for the 911 call to be made. And I *heard* it being made. Bottom line, if Ellie Bray's alive, she has me to thank for it."

He looks at me curiously. "Who made the call?"

"A young lady."

He waits till I say: "Jackie Fish."

"Odd name."

"Odd girl."

"You think she'll corroborate your story to the police?"

"Possibly."

"You have her number?"

"Why do you care?"

"I think you should call her. Before the police arrive."

"Have they been summoned?"

"Not yet. But just to be clear, you *do* have Jackie's phone number, correct?"

"Uh...not exactly."

"Would you *like* to have it? Exactly?" He hands me a folded slip of paper with Jackie's name and number.

"How could you possibly—"

"Give her a call."

I stare at the number and shake my head. "If you know this much, I'm sure you know we went our separate ways."

"Call her anyway."

I hesitate. Then say, "You're trying to set me up."

"How so?"

"If this is her actual number, and I call it from my cell phone, the police will have a direct link to me."

"Call her anyway," he says. Then adds, "I insist."

I call the number and listen as it rings softly in the ear piece a split second, then loudly *behind* me! I turn to find Jackie Fish standing in the doorway that leads to the kitchen. She's chewing on a raw carrot, saying, "Eh...what's up, Doc?"

Chapter 20

I CAN'T DENY I'm surprised.

I look Jackie over, searching for signs of injury. Seeing none, I take a moment to reflect on how simple my life is when Creed's not around. Then say, "I guess the drop-off at Inspiration Point is overrated."

Jackie says, "The initial drop is only five feet, to a narrow ledge. Then it gets worse. But...you didn't even *look*! What sort of person watches a woman jump off a cliff and drives away without even *checking* on her?"

Creed says, "A guilty one."

I shrug. "All's well that ends well," I say. "The relevant part of this is Jackie can corroborate my 911 call."

"How so?" Creed says.

"She's the one who made it."

They look at each other as if confused. Then Creed says, "Have you not yet figured out that Jackie called *me*?"

It takes me a moment: "She works for *you*?"

"Today she did."

"What does that mean?"

"She's not a regular."

I look at Jackie. "You're what, an actress?"

Creed says, "She's a normal person who owes me a favor. A small one, not like yours."

I take a split-second to mentally review my earlier encounter with Jackie through this new filter and come up with more questions than answers. "What did you make her do?" I ask. "Because she sure as hell didn't fulfil her sexual promises."

Jackie rolls her eyes.

Creed says, "Her job was to plant evidence."

"Where?"

"In the car you stole."

"What sort of evidence?"

"The kind that can ruin your life."

Noting the confused look on my face he says, "Jackie? You told him the story, didn't you?"

She nods.

He says, "Tell it again."

"No need," I say. "She was fucking her best-friend's husband, a golfer, under a tree at the base of a cliff, which I'm now assuming was Inspiration Point. He was on top, pounding away, when suddenly his head blew up. Ridiculous."

"True story," Creed says.

I roll my eyes. "Let's say it is. How can it ruin my life?"

"You know what makes a good story great, Doc?"

"What's that?"

"Point of view."

"Am I supposed to know what you're talking about?"

"Jackie told the story from *her* point of view. The part that affected her: she fucked her best friend's husband outdoors, under a tree, at the bottom of a cliff. And his head appeared to blow up. After realizing her lover was dead, she freaked out. Grabbed her clothes and started running. Got to her car before coming to the conclusion there was no immediate threat to her safety. No one was chasing her, but the spot she'd been making love would soon become a crime scene, and she didn't want to be involved.

"She got dressed, grabbed the flashlight she keeps in her glove box, and the jacket she keeps in her trunk, then bravely retraced her steps to the spot the lovemaking took place. She searched the entire area for any personal evidence she might have left, and didn't find anything that could tie her to the guy. But she did find a bloody gun, and realized someone had thrown it high out over the cliff, where it fell through the tree without hitting a single limb, and crashed onto her lover's head at the very moment he lifted his face upward, in ecstasy."

"Such a romantic story," I say. "And from her point of view, his head *appeared* to explode."

"That's right. Jackie didn't know what to do, so she picked the gun up by the barrel and wrapped her jacket around it and went home."

"Who threw the gun?"

Creed smiles. "Same story, different point of view. I understand you're Mr. C's personal physician?"

"Who told you *that*?"

"He did."

"That was a temporary situation. We've parted ways. Amicably."

Creed laughs. "Mr. C's a mafia kingpin."

"So?"

"It ain't over till he says it's over."

"Yeah, well he said it was over."

"When's the last time you spoke to him?"

"Months ago."

"Well, as of yesterday, he still considers you his personal physician."

I frown.

This isn't good.

I ask, "What does Mr. C have to do with Jackie Fish?"

"One of his goons shot a guy, put him in a car, and set it on fire. Drove the car a distance, saw the drop off at Inspiration Point, got out and hurled the gun over the cliff. The gun flew through the air, hit Jackie's boyfriend in the head. She wrapped the gun—the murder weapon—in her jacket, took it home, wiped her prints off the barrel, placed it in a plastic bag, and put it in her purse. Next day she heard about the guy who got shot in the burning car 20 miles away and wondered if the gun that killed her boyfriend happened to be the murder weapon. When the cops announced the burning car incident appeared to be an organized crime hit, Jackie called a friend who called me, and the rest is history."

"You can't just say the rest is history. The rest is still evolving."

"Good point. Anyway, here's the deal: Jackie contacted me a few days ago, and I just happened to be following you at the time, trying to figure out how to motivate you to help me with my terrorist problem. My original plan: she'd come on to you at the hospital, work her way into your car or home for sex, during which time she'd plant the gun."

I laugh. "That's not much of a threat."

"No?"

"I guarantee the shooter didn't leave any fingerprints on the gun, and I know *I* didn't, so the police wouldn't have much of a case against me."

"I wouldn't tell the cops about the gun. I'd tell Mr. C."

Brilliant plan, because "Mr. C would think I kept the gun to set him up."

"Exactly. So that was the original plan. But then you stole Judson Bray's Porsche and gave us more options."

As I think it through I realize Jackie played me perfectly. She insisted being alone in the Porsche to make the call to 911 and asked me to stand 10 feet away, with my head turned, so I wouldn't make her nervous. But in reality she was buying time to plant the gun in Bray's car. Then she pretended to call 911, but actually called Creed. Still, there's something I don't understand, so I ask: "I get that you were following me when I took Judson's Porsche. But how did you know I'd stop at the tavern? And how did you get Jackie there so quickly?"

Creed says, "See? This is what makes you so difficult to understand."

"What do you mean?"

"We've been talking all this time, and you know I've had a team following you. You know Jackie called *me*, not 911, and now you're asking about the logistics of getting Jackie to the tavern in time to manipulate you into letting her plant evidence."

"So?"

"You haven't even thought to ask about Ellie Bray."

"What about her?"

"Aren't you concerned about her?"

"Not particularly."

"Why not?"

I shrug.

He says, "You spent 40 minutes saving her life and sewing her up with what my people call the most brilliant surgical technique they've ever seen. You seriously don't care if she survived?"

"Not really."

"Are you the least bit curious where she is?"

"I assume your people took her to a hospital. If they didn't, then yeah, I suppose I ought to be curious."

"We drove her to a heliport, then air-lifted her to our private hospital at Sensory Resources. Do you want to know her condition?"

I shrug.

He says, "She's holding her own." He pauses. "I don't get it."

"What's that?"

"You're a doctor. You took the time to treat her. But if you're being honest with me right now, you never cared if she survived."

"I didn't and don't."

"How's that possible?"

"I only care about the kids I treat."

"Why?"

"You wouldn't understand."

"Try me."

"They're innocent."

He gives me a long look, then says, "I think you just told me you're not planning to keep the promise you made."

"I can't believe I'm saying this, but if Salib's kid gets as far as my operating room, I'm going to save him."

"Even if it means tens of thousands of people will die?"

"That's right."

"You're probably the only doctor in the world who could save this kid."

"Depending on what you do to make him critically ill, I expect you're right."

"If I kill you, some other doctor will botch the case, and we're home free."

"True. But according to you, I'm useful to your future somehow."

"I suppose I could hold you hostage until the crisis passes."

"If you do, I'll never cooperate with you, ever again."

He looks at Jackie a minute, then back at me and says, "Let's go for a ride."

"Me too?" Jackie says.

"Yeah."

"I thought I was done," she says.

"You're the alibi, assuming Gideon cooperates."

She says, "Are you really gonna make him kill an innocent kid?"

Creed takes a deep breath. "All kids are innocent at that age, Jackie. Including the dozens or hundreds who'll die in the terrorist strike if I lose the opportunity to kill Salib. And as I've told Box numerous times, I'm not asking him to *kill* this child, I'm simply asking him not to save him."

Jackie looks at me. "He makes a compelling case, Doc. I agree it's an awful situation, but if you look at it another way, by not helping this one child, you're saving hundreds more."

Creed says, "Thank you, Jackie."

I frown. "Don't let him bullshit you, Jackie. He's asking more than he's letting on."

"What do you mean?"

"After I make sure the kid dies, Creed wants me to plant a bomb in his dead body and sew it in place."

Jackie does a double-take, looks at Creed for confirmation, gets it in the form of a shrug, then says, "I can't be part of this."

"Too late," he says. "You're in it to win it. Let's go."

Chapter 21

THANKFULLY, CREED DOESN'T force us to climb behind the washing machine and use my so-called "back entrance." We leave the conventional way, out the front door
to the elevator, and as we exit the building, Joe the
Doorman doesn't ask why three of us are leaving when only
one of us entered a few minutes ago. I guess that's because
Joe's the night guy, and would have no way of knowing if
Creed and Jackie entered before his shift started. But it *does*
highlight a security risk I never knew existed.

A security risk that Creed spotted instantly, more than
three years ago.

Creed's driver collects us in front of my building and
takes us to the financial district, where Creed points out the
block where he believes the attack will take place.

"Why here?" Jackie asks.

"It's the hardest to patrol. But the attack could be any
of these city blocks."

His driver takes us to view the other possible targets so I'll have a better understanding how impossible it is to protect the entire area, and help me understand the enormous devastation the city would experience if Salib isn't stopped.

"I understand why you're concerned," I say. "But you don't even know for certain there'll be an attack."

"We have an informant."

"Our hospital gets bomb threats all the time."

"This is different," he says, with rising impatience.

"How?"

Creed's glaring at me and I know why: I'm wasting precious time he needs to devote to other issues. He's accustomed to doing things his way and not having to explain himself. I get that, I'm the same way. When I'm working on a dying infant I don't have the time, desire, or patience to explain myself to the nurses who are there to help me. I want their cooperation, not their input. So I understand how difficult this is for Creed. But for some reason he's giving me these detailed explanations, and all I can think is he must need me for something really important down the line.

I prod him for a response to my question: "How are our hospital's threats different than your intel?"

He says, "People who call in threats to your hospital fall into specific categories: a former patient whose surgery got botched. The guy who received the insanely high hospital bill you sent for his wife's treatment. They're angry, and want to punish you by disrupting your business. Or maybe the caller is part of that quarter-percent of humanity that gets off on watching people of authority fear for their lives. Or he might be unemployed, and wants to experience the satisfaction of forcing the doctors, nurses, and hospital personnel to evacuate their building and abandon their jobs, if only temporarily."

"What's the difference between those people and your informant?"

"Threat assessment."

"What's that mean?"

"When your hospital gets a bomb threat, one of your staff members has been trained to evaluate the risk based on specific criteria. And if not, he or she knows who to call. It's nearly always a hoax, and in 80% of those cases your specialist will know the odds of attack prior to ordering an evacuation of the building. But if an informant calls with credible information, and passes every part of the evaluation process, including naming names...the building gets evacuated. But even then the odds of a real threat are virtually zero."

"What makes *your* informant so credible?"

"It's Salib's father."

"No shit?" Jackie says.

"He loves his son, but can't abide genocide."

"He'd let you kill his son?"

"I promised I'd capture him."

"You lied."

He shrugs.

As I shake my head, Creed adds, "If Salib isn't stopped, thousands of men, women, and children will be killed, and those deaths will cause exponential suffering for their families. Dozens of major businesses will go bankrupt, or be shut down for months, forcing thousands of workers to be unemployed. A victory for Salib ensures that around the world, thousands of men and women will be emboldened to join terrorist groups to wage war on the United States. Gideon, you won't believe this, but I don't want Salib's son to die any more than you do. But my job routinely comes down to these types of decisions, and I have no doubt this is the best chance we have to protect our country from this attack."

"Then why not kill the kid yourself?"

"I'd do it in a heartbeat if I thought it would flush Salib out of hiding. Unfortunately, if his son dies mysteriously, he won't show. He'll suspect we're onto him. But if his kid develops a high fever, vomiting, diarrhea, and gets progressively worse with each passing hour, and if his family takes him to your hospital and the world famous Doctor Gideon Box personally treats him—Salib will have no reason to believe he's being set up. That's why it has to be *you* taking care of the kid. Everyone knows you've never lost a patient. When the kid dies, Salib will accept it as God's will, and he'll want to pray over him."

"And you'll blow him up, along with his family, friends, and terror cell members."

"Exactly."

I think about all this and come to the conclusion he's right. It's a tough call, but the kid has to die.

"Okay," I say, surprising myself.

He looks me in the eyes and tells me to say I won't allow Salib's son to live.

I do, and this time I can tell he's convinced I mean it.

...But I don't.

While I understand and agree with everything Creed said, I'm simply not going to allow a dying kid to succumb, regardless of the reason. But Creed doesn't have to know that right now.

"When is this going to take place?" I ask.

"Which part?"

"Salib's son."

"It's already started."

"What? You told me he was fine!"

"Sorry. I should have said he *appears* to be fine."

"How long before he's critical?"

"Twenty-four hours, give or take."

Shit!

Feeling his eyes boring in on me, I say, "I'll make sure he doesn't live. You have my word."

With genuine sincerity Creed says, "Thanks, Gideon. I know this isn't easy for you."

No shit!

As we head back to my place, Creed places a call. After hanging up he says, "Why's Judson still in the hospital?"

"He shouldn't be. He's been discharged. Are you sure he's still there?"

"I've got a guy watching his car. It's still in the parking space where you left it."

I frown. "Maybe his condition deteriorated."

Creed says, "We need him to be in his car when you call Mr. C."

"*What?* Why the hell would *I* call Mr. C?"

"To tell him while under the influence of the drugs you administered, Judson confessed."

"To what?"

"Having the gun. The murder weapon."

"Mr. C will *kill* him!"

"Better him than *you*, right?"

"But Judson didn't *do* anything!"

Creed cocks his head. "Can you possibly be that naïve?"

"About what?"

"Judson's not *ill*, Gideon. He's been using the ER as his alibi."

"For what?"

"Killing his wife."

"How could you possibly know that?"

"Who do you think slit her throat?"

I look him over carefully. "Not you. No way!"

"Why not?"

"If *you* took the contract, she'd be dead."

He smiles. "Judson knows I'm an assassin, but he made the mistake many make during the hiring process."

"What's that?"

"He's seen too many movies and TV shows, and didn't want to say too much, in case he was being taped. So he used ridiculous code words. In the movies the hitmen always read between the lines, so that was Judson's frame of reference when he told me on the phone that our code word would be Hofstra."

"Why Hofstra?"

"That's where his wife went to college. So we met in a parking lot, and when I approached his car I had to say 'Hofstra,' before he'd let me in. Then he said, 'You went to Hofstra? Do you know my wife?' And I said, 'I'm not sure. What was her maiden name?' He got me to say 'Yeah, I remember her.' I pointed out how gorgeous she was, and played that whole bullshit game until he handed me a slip of paper with his address and said I should feel free to stop by their house sometime and pay Ellie a *visit*. I played along and asked if I should bring anything, and he took his finger and slid it across his throat. Later on, after he felt comfortable with me I asked, 'Just to be clear, you want me to slash her throat, correct?' He nodded, and *assumed* that would result in her death."

I rub my face with both hands. Then say, "You couldn't have known I'd steal his car and drive to her house."

"Why not?"

"Because *I* didn't know I was going to! I saw the keys, saw Ellie's photo, and made a snap decision. It wasn't planned. What are you grinning at?"

"Have you ever seen a magician tell a person to pick a card, then tell the person which card he picked?"

I say nothing, so he continues: "The magician forced the card into the person's hand."

"If you're trying to claim you somehow tricked me into stealing Judson's car, you're deeply underestimating me."

"I never underestimate people. Especially those with 180 IQ's."

"So now you're a magician?"

"No. In the example I gave, the magician forced the card into the audience member's hand. I simply forced your hand."

"How?"

"I know what motivates you. I lined those things up for you on a silver platter, and let your brain make the connection."

"I have no idea what you're trying to say."

"I told Judson to fake a heart attack and go to your hospital's emergency room at a specific time, which I knew was close to the end of your shift. I told him to ask for you, specifically. I told him to leave his car keys in plain sight, and make sure his phone was programmed with Ellie's picture and phone number on speed dial. Then I told him to make sure *you* called Ellie, not him. Later on, when the police determine Ellie's time of death, you'd become Judson's alibi."

"Because I spoke to her on the phone moments before her murder, while Judson was in the exam room."

"That's right, but here's the kicker: Judson didn't know and *still* doesn't know that Ellie's alive. But when this Salib thing is over, she *is* going to die. The only question is, who's going to prison for her death? Judson or you?"

"Why me?"

"I installed pinhole cameras in Judson's garage, hallway, and kitchen; and in both closets, and their master bathroom. My guys are editing the tape to show you drove his car into the garage, searched his house from top to bottom, and even stole underwear from Ellie's dresser. I've also got the most amazing footage that shows you counting out several thousand dollars you stole from Judson's closet."

"I didn't take that money!"

"You think the cops will believe that?" He reaches into his pocket and shows me the cash. Then says, "Best of all, we've got video footage of you leaning over Ellie's body to check her pulse, then rushing out the room, running down the hall, and into the garage."

"I was getting my medical bag!"

"*Really?* I wonder why *that* footage never made it to the copy I saw! Maybe it got lost on the cutting room floor. But we did get some nice shots of you wiping down all the surfaces in the closets before driving away. My geeks will splice that into the final tape in the proper sequence. Bottom line, it was all planned out. Judson's wife dies, you're his alibi. Refuse my favor, you become his wife's murderer."

"What about the stitches?"

He says nothing, so I add, "The stitches will prove I tried to save Ellie's life."

He says, "There won't be any stitches in her neck when the police find her body."

"Great. All that work I did to save her life was for nothing."

"Sorry."

"And I'm supposed to believe you assumed I'd steal Judson's car and drive to his house?"

"I didn't assume it. I *knew* it."

"How?"

"Same reason you know you can save this child before you even see him: you're a student of medicine."

"And what are you?"

"A student of people."

"You've studied me."

"That's right."

"And you knew I'd steal his car, go to his house, and save Ellie's life."

"Not exactly. I knew you'd steal his car and go straight to his house. I wasn't sure you'd help Ellie."

"You were testing me."

He nods.

"You wanted to see how I'd react in that situation."

"And how you'd respond."

"What's the difference?"

"I wanted to see what type of decisions you'd make."

"Why do you give a shit?"

"I want to know what type of person you are in a clutch."

"Why?"

"I have plans for you."

For a few seconds, we just look at each other. Then I say, "What if I *hadn't* helped Ellie?"

"My medical team would have stepped in."

"What medical team?"

"Who do you think kept Ellie alive till you got there?"

"How many?"

"Three."

"Where *were* they?"

"In the basement, in the wine cellar, waiting for my cue."

"This is insane! Why go to this much trouble?"

He shrugs. "I can't predict your future behavior without studying your past and present actions."

"Remarkable. Except for one thing: now that you've told me all this, I can purposely alter my future behavior to be less predictable."

He smiles and hands me a slip of paper that says: *I'll just change my behavior and be less predictable from now on.*

Unbelievable.

"Not my exact words," I say.

"Close enough."

I shake my head. It's just too much. Thank God I have a secret weapon. I happen to know the one person on earth who can protect me from Creed after I fuck him over...

...If only she will.

Chapter 22

WHEN THE DRIVER pulls to a stop in front of my building Creed says, "Be strong, Gideon."

I nod. "Donovan?"

"Yeah?"

"You're not going to share that video of me and Bruce's wife, are you?"

"Not if I don't have to."

I nod, exit the car, and keep walking till I'm in the lobby, facing Joe the Doorman, who's grinning at me like I brought him a gift. I know what's coming. Sure enough, he makes the funny voice and says: "What's up Doc?" -and bursts into laughter. "Get it? Bugs Bunny?" He laughs again. "I can't believe I never thought to say that before!"

Actually, Joe says it to me at least once a month. Then forgets. Now he's saying, "I bet people say that to you all the time!"

"Nope."

"Well, they should!"

"Perish the thought. Can I ask a favor?"

"Want me to say it again?"

"No."

He frowns.

"I was hoping to use your phone. It's urgent."

"What happened to yours?" he says.

"I don't know. It just stopped working."

He holds out his palm, says, "I'm great with phones. Let me take a look."

Realizing this isn't going to work the way I hoped, I say "Okay, you busted me. Here's the thing: my phone's fine, but there's this lady, and—"

"Say no more! Let me guess: you don't want her husband to see your number on Caller ID."

I smile. "I can't confirm that, since you told me to say no more."

"But that's it, isn't it! You sly dog! She's hot, isn't she?"

I shrug.

He says, "I bet she's hotter than a ghost pepper's ass. Wow! Must be nice. I should've studied harder in school."

He hands me his phone and says, "He's not gonna come after *me*, is he?"

"Who?"

"The husband."

"No, this is a one-time, two-minute call. She'll tell him it was a telemarketer, or wrong number."

I hold the phone in my palm and stare at him till he says, "Oh. Sorry. I suppose I ought to give you some privacy."

"Thanks, Joe."

Chapter 23

SHE ANSWERS THE phone curtly: "State your name, please."

"It's me. Gideon Box."

"*Gideon?*" She hesitates before saying, "Whose phone is this?"

"My doorman's."

"Well, *this* should be an entertaining story! Let's hear it."

"I'm in trouble."

She laughs. "*There's* a shock! What's happened this time?"

"You know Donovan Creed."

She pauses. "What about him?"

"He wants me to kill someone."

"Who?"

"An infant."

"Was this a random request, or did he give you a good reason?"

"National Security. It all boils down to the greater good theory."

"That sounds like Creed. Whose kid are we talking about?"

"Some terrorist's."

She laughs. "If I wanted to kill a terrorist's child, I'd hire Creed."

"What's your point?"

"Why you?"

"I owe him a favor."

"Well, that says it all. Want my opinion?"

"No. I want your help."

She laughs. "You'll get my opinion anyway: kill the kid, Gideon. Trust me, you'll thank me later."

"I can't do it."

"Have you told Creed that?"

"Yeah. But when he threatened my life I gave in and told him I would."

"But you're not going to?"

"No."

"Then you really do have a problem."

"That's what I've been trying to tell you. Can you help me?"

"Of course."

"Will you?"

"That depends. What do you have in mind?"

"Protection."

"From Creed?"

"Yeah. And his people."

"For how long?"

"Forever."

She laughs. "I'd have to kill him."

I breathe a sigh of relief. "I *knew* you'd understand."

Chapter 24

"I'M NOT GOING to kill Creed for you," she says.

"Why not?"

"I need him. At least for the time being."

"Why?"

She goes quiet for 20 seconds before saying, "You know better than to ask me personal questions, correct?"

"Yes, absolutely! I didn't realize what I—"

"I answered one, for old time's sake. But then you asked a second. I can't believe you have the balls to ask me two questions about my personal business."

"You're right. Again, I'm sorry."

"I don't owe you *anything*, Gideon. I answer to no one."

"I know. It's just—I'm under a lot of stress here, and...I'm truly sorry."

"You're the one asking for favors here, not me."

"Quite right. I apologize."

She goes quiet a full minute, then another, and another. I know she's waiting to see if I'll break the silence, and if I do, she'll end the call. After what seems an eternity she says, "I assume you've put together some sort of plan?"

"I have."

"Very well. I'll hear you out, then make my decision."

"About killing him?"

"About protecting you."

"That's fair. When can we meet?"

"When do you need me?"

"Immediately."

"Okay. I'm available."

"When?"

"Right now. Come on up."

"What do you mean?"

"Come on up."

"Where?"

"Your place."

"I'm sorry...*what?*"

"I'm in your penthouse."

"You're...*excuse me?*"

"Upstairs. In your penthouse."

"How's that possible?"

"I used the back entrance."

What the *fuck?* Am I the only person in town who doesn't know about my back entrance? "When did you *get* here?"

"This morning."

"You're shitting me, right? I mean, how do you even know where I *am* right now?"

"You're in the lobby. How else could you be using Joe the Doorman's phone?"

"You've been at my place all *day?*"

"That's right."

"Why?"

She pauses, then says, "Can you really be that stupid?"

"What do you mean?"

"I told you not to ask me personal questions. This conversation is over."

I try to apologize, but find myself talking to a dead phone. I race across the lobby, give Joe's phone back to him, jump in the elevator, ride it to the top floor. Seconds later, I'm running through my penthouse, calling her name: "*Rose!*"

Chapter 25

REMEMBER WHEN I said there are three people whose calls I always have to take? One is Creed, the assassin; the second is Mr. C, the mobster; and the third, Rose Stout, is sitting atop my kitchen counter.

Rose is drop dead gorgeous.

And 300 years old.

And...she's a witch.

I know what you're thinking: you don't believe in witches. You want to read books and watch TV shows that are realistic. Things that happen in my life can be "out there," but they have to be plausible, or you can't "go there," right?

Right.

And then you tell me I need to watch your favorite TV shows: *The Walking Dead* (Zombies), and *Game of Thrones* (Zombies, Witches, Shape-Shifters, Magicians, Dragons, etc.) or you like the new *Supergirl* (she flies and has super powers) and you go to the theater to watch movies about werewolves and vampires and gorgeous women who want to be tied up and enjoy being teased and tortured, and want to have non-stop sex, and...where was I?

Oh yeah. The witch.

Rose has witchy abilities.

And she's 100% real.

So get over it.

My phone rings. It's Creed. I put him on speaker so Rose can hear.

He says, "Why am I getting white noise out of your apartment?"

"I don't know what you're talking about."

"No sounds, no visual. You can't have dismantled the cameras and microphones this quickly."

I look at Rose. She smiles. To Creed I say, "You bugged my home?"

"Not recently. By the way, you lied."

"About what?"

"My guy's been working on the video feed for your operating room, and guess what he discovered?"

"There isn't one?"

"That's right. And you know why?"

"It's the one room in the hospital where the operations aren't taped."

"Exactly. Care to explain?"

"The hospital doesn't want any video evidence floating around that shows how I treat my patients while trying to save them."

"How'd you manage that?"

"By saving them. The parents are happy to get a live child back, so no one complains. Except the nurses, of course."

"Care to explain why you lied to me about the operations being taped?"

"At the time I said that, I was trying to discourage you. Then later, after agreeing to let Salib's kid die, it slipped my mind. I forgot to set you straight about it."

"Well, no harm no foul. It's one less problem I have to solve." He pauses a moment, then says, "I found out why Judson hasn't left the hospital."

"And why is that?"

"He's dead."

"*What?*"

"He went to the bathroom to take a shit, locked the door, sat on the pot and suffered a stroke. No one knew he was in there, and when they finally broke in, he was dead."

"That's...*insane!*"

"Helluva way to go, right?"

"You're certain it was Judson?"

"My guys don't waste my time with rumors."

"Where is he now?"

"Hospital Morgue. Guess you don't have to call Mr. C."

"Shouldn't I tell Mr. C about the gun?"

"Only if you're tired of being his personal physician."

"What do you mean?"

"The police will find it when they search his car. With any luck they'll trace it to Mr. C's goon. They'll bring him in, cut him a deal. When he talks, Mr. C goes to prison."

"The police won't search his car if he died from a stroke."

"You're forgetting about Ellie. Sooner or later someone's going to file a missing person report. Judson's car will be sitting in the parking spot where you left it. The cops will search it for clues and find the gun."

"That sounds great except for one thing," I say.

"What's that?"

"Mr. C's goons would never use a gun that can be traced."

"They don't need a registration if they've got fingerprints."

"What are you talking about?"

"The goon's fingerprints are all over the gun."

"That would never happen."

"Not without my help, you mean."

"You transferred the goon's prints to the *gun?*"

"I did."

"But how's that *possible?*"

"I'm Donovan Creed."

Chapter 26

BEFORE I HAVE a chance to tell Rose my plan, my phone rings again. This time it's Bruce Luce, and I'm thinking either Truth said something about our visit, or Creed sent him video proof I molested his wife.

Or both.

Thankfully, it's neither.

He says, "Two things, Gideon: first, you're on call. I've already notified your team."

"Why?"

"I just accepted a request to admit an infant with life-threatening symptoms."

"Who's the kid?"

"Does it matter?"

"It does to me."

"Just a sec." He shuffles some papers. Then says, "Baqir Salib."

I take a deep breath. It's started.

"Casey's on duty," I say. "Let him handle this one."

"How many times have you complained that Casey's a quack?"

"Eighty-two."

"There you go. And anyway, the kid's family asked for you specifically, and said all the right things."

"Like what?"

"Like price is no object."

"Bruce?"

"Yeah?"

"You're a whore."

"That may be, but I run a helluva great hospital. And speaking of whores, you've got the sweetest deal in town. Think of this as an opportunity to prove you're worth the exorbitant salary we pay you for a precious few hours of effort each month."

"Where's the kid now?"

"Breighton Medical. He'll probably be fine, but you need to be ready in the event he responds negatively to whatever treatment they're giving him."

"What's his issue?"

"Uncontrollable vomiting, severe diarrhea, dehydration, possible seizure...and a host of other things."

"He's probably been poisoned."

"I'm recording this conversation, you know."

"Of course you are. What's the second thing you planned to tell me?"

"Tomorrow morning, eight a.m., a group of elderly people will be touring our hospital."

"How could that possibly affect *me*?"

"Their first stop is your office."

"Not a chance."

He laughs, unable to control his glee. "Sorry, Gideon. It's been worked out in advance."

"By whom?"

"One of the board members."

"When was *this* decided?"

"Monday."

"And you're just *now* telling me?"

"That's right. I knew you wouldn't mind."

"You just said I'm on call. I can't meet a bunch of dried up geezers."

"That's *exactly* why you can! You'll be in your office anyway. Assuming you're not in surgery, you'll host the seniors."

"Why?"

"They love you."

"Fuck you, Bruce!"

He laughs. "Go figure, right? Apparently, they read an article about your work with children and wanted to meet you. So they contacted the hospital and got passed around until someone on the Board said you'd be delighted to explain the ins and outs of emergency room procedures."

"That makes no sense."

"Sure it does. Our lawyers won't allow you to talk about how you terrorize your infant patients, so we had to come up with a different subject. If you upset them when discussing the ER we can always cover by saying you don't *work* in the ER and therefore your comments—whatever they are—shouldn't be taken literally."

"Which board member authorized this bullshit meeting?"

"Good question. Um...let me think a minute. Oh, that's right: I believe it was me."

"You're an asshole!"

"Well, this is fun. Your recorded response to saving a child's life was to call your boss a whore. Your response to motivating senior citizens to choose our emergency room over the competition was to call your boss an asshole. Would you like to amplify your remarks?"

"Yeah. Go fuck yourself."

"You're making this so easy for me."

"I think Baqir Salib has been poisoned."

"So you said. If you get a chance to work on him you can start with that premise."

"I will. As for the old folks? You've got a dozen people on staff who can give them that lecture, and a tour to boot. Their being in my office could interfere with my ability to do my job correctly."

"Oh, lighten up, Gideon. What's the big deal? Unlike the rest of the world, these senior citizens actually *like* you. Give them a thrill. Tell them about our facilities. Make them want to come here when they get sick."

"I don't get it. You know I suck at that sort of thing."

"*Do* you? Well, just do your best."

It suddenly hits me: "You *want* me to fuck this up."

"Don't be silly."

"You're setting me up, hoping I'll say something that'll get back to the Board."

"If the Board gets any feedback, I'm sure it will be quite complimentary."

"Fuck you, Bruce."

He laughs and hangs up.

Rose says, "What an asshole! No wonder you fingered his wife!"

I frown. "Is there no privacy in my own home?"

Chapter 27

IT TAKES FIVE minutes to tell Rose what Creed expects me to do to Salib's kid, five more to tell her why, and another five to explain my plan: since Rose is my former surgical assistant, she'll be in the operating room with me when Salib's kid is wheeled in. If Creed happens to show up, she'll freeze him in place until he's no longer a threat.

A brief note: like you, me, and most people you know, Rose has several unique talents. Unlike us, one of them is the ability to freeze people in place. (If we're being technical, "Freezing" isn't the accurate term, since there's no actual lowering of body temperature. The way Rose explains it, she slows people's movements to the extent it appears they're frozen in place.)

You're probably wondering how long it lasts. The answer is I don't know. Rose has frozen two people I know about: Callie Carpenter (who works for Creed) and my former girlfriend, Amelia Chambers, whom she froze in my bedroom long enough to have sex with me (Rose had sex with me, not Amelia). Not that you asked, but the sex was *incredible*. This, because like I say, Rose is a witch, and also because Amelia was right there while it happened. But my relationship with Amelia went in the shitter when I found that despite being "frozen" she was completely aware of everything happening around her. Amelia took exception to watching Rose and I have sex, not to mention hearing the disparaging comments I made regarding her mental health and lovemaking skills.

So if Creed shows up at the hospital, Rose will subdue him till we can spirit Baqir Salib to the ICU, at which point we'll tell his family he's expected to make a full recovery. Meanwhile, Rose will stand guard over Baqir until his father tries to blow up Wall Street. He won't succeed of course, because I'm sure Creed has some sort of backup plan that will keep him so busy he won't have time to worry about exacting revenge on me. And since he needs me for something big in the future, he'll probably keep me around until I can do whatever it is he wants. Maybe I'll do such a good job he'll forgive me for saving Salib's kid. But if not, I'll be ready.

Creed thinks he can threaten me with the severity of the torture, and says it's the *way* he's going to kill me that makes all the difference. But what he doesn't know is before going to bed tonight (and every day thereafter) I'm going to attach a tiny (nearly microscopic) water-tight capsule to the outside of my #31 tooth every day. The capsule will contain several drops of liquid nicotine, one of the world's most lethal poisons. The moment Creed tries to subdue or torture me, I'll scratch off the capsule, crunch it between my teeth, and die before he has any idea what happened. If he somehow manages to bind my hands before I can scratch it off, I'll wait for him to punch me in the cheek. That should kill me. If he doesn't punch me, I'll use my tongue to work it free, then bite it. And if none of that happens, I'll only have to hang on for 12 to 18 hours, because by then the capsule will dissolve into my gum on its own, and I'll die a quick, easy death.

I can deal with that.

Rose asks, "What if Creed doesn't show himself prior to surgery? I can't disable him if I can't see him."

"No problem. If he fails to show, we'll do the surgery, then pass Baqir off to one of our nurses, and you'll run interference while she wheels him to ICU."

"And if his people show up in numbers?"

"Can you freeze everyone you and the nurse encounter until you get to ICU?"

"I don't see why not."

I give her a thumbs-up.

She says, "One last thing: if Creed gets by me somehow, do you have a plan B?"

"I do."

"Want to share it with me?"

"No."

She shrugs. "Fair enough. But whatever it is, it's on you."

"Of course!"

She looks at me a moment. "If he brings Callie Carpenter to the party, we could have trouble."

"Why? You froze her before, outside the Four Seasons Restaurant."

"I did. But just barely."

I frown. "Just barely ought to be good enough."

"I'm sure I can deal with Creed or Callie. But both could be a problem. Especially if there are others milling about."

"Just do your best. Like I say, I've got a backup plan."

Chapter 28

IT'S 8:00 A.M., AND thirteen old people are in my conference room. Eight sitting, five standing, all talking. When I
enter, all hell breaks loose. The sitting ones jump to their
feet and join the others crowding around me like I'm the
conquering hero returning home to greet the king. The
women are hugging and flirting, and the men are backslap-
ping me and trying to shake my hand. I make a mental note
to get a copy of whatever article it was they read about me.

They swarm, touching and hugging, and after tolerating
as much as I can handle, I hold up my arms and say, "I've
been asked to talk about what to expect when you come to
our emergency room for treatment."

Realizing the talk is about to begin, the eight ladies
quickly reclaim their seats, and the men move back to keep
from obstructing their view. When all are settled I say,
"When Mr. Luce scheduled this visit he had no way of
knowing I'd be on call this morning, so I'll apologize in

advance for making this brief. I've just been informed a critically ill infant is being transported to our hospital even as we speak. He's been receiving care at an area hospital, but his condition has steadily deteriorated to the point they're passing him on to me. In about a half hour I'll attempt to save his life."

"God bless you, doctor!" one of them says. The others amen.

"Thank you. Let's get started. Every year 120 million Americans visit an emergency room. At some point in your lives—and soon, judging from your ages—each of you will do the same. I'd like to tell you it'll be a pleasant experience, but that would be a lie."

Several ladies frown.

I continue: "Your visit will begin in triage, where a nurse will evaluate your condition and assign you a number from one to three, with one being the worst. If you're a three it means you're not in danger of dying immediately. That's the good news. The bad news is you'll have to wait up to 48 hours to receive treatment."

The women are gasping, the men's eyes are bugging out, so I say, "That's worst case. The average wait is four hours, so remember to bring a book or iPad, or whatever. While you're here, we'll run tests you won't understand and may not need. Some will be run to protect us from the lawsuits your family will file if we maim or kill you; some will be run because we need the money; and some will be run because we actually think they might help you.

"After triage, we'll put you in an examination room, where you'll have to strip naked. I know that won't be fun for some of you, but try not to be modest. Accept the fact we're going to see everything you brought to the party."

"Don't we get a gown?" a lady asks.

"Yes. But if we want to see your woohoo, it's going to happen. You'll be poked, prodded, tested, questioned, and re-questioned. We'll explain what we plan to do, but we'll underplay the dangers, because if we told you everything that could go wrong you'd haul your asses out of here and take your chances on the street."

"Can we refuse to sign the forms?" someone says.

"Yes, but if you do we won't treat you."

"Why?"

"Because those forms give us the right to kill you."

One guy says, "I'm told your doctors and nurses are the best in the city."

"Really? Who told you *that*?"

"Mr. Luce."

Of course he did.

I nod. "Well, our doctors and nurses are as good as you'll find anywhere, but since you wanted the truth, let me put it this way: how much did *you* learn in school when studying four years of French?"

"Spanish," he says. Then adds, "Not much."

"Your emergency room physicians attended four years of med school, one year as an intern, and two or three years in residency."

"That's pretty comprehensive."

"True. But here's the real test: if you're an ER physician, and the only thing keeping you from being certified by the American Board of Emergency Medicine is a two-day oral and written test, wouldn't you take it?"

"Of course."

"Me too," I say. "But only if I felt confident of *passing*. Therefore, is it just me, or does it bother you that half of all ER physicians aren't certified?"

It's not just me. They look positively miserable.

A lady asks, "Can you give us some tips?"

"As a matter of fact, I can. Tip number one: if your emergency is chest pain, possible stroke, poisoning, serious trauma or infection, or anything you consider life-threatening, get to the ER sooner, not later. But for lesser problems, if you avoid nights, weekends, and holidays, you'll not only be seen quicker, but according to surveys you'll leave happier. Except for Mondays."

"What happens on Mondays?"

"You don't want to know. Tip two: life-threatening bacteria can live on hospital surfaces for weeks, so make sure anyone who touches you washes their hands first. Tip three: be nice to everyone you encounter, because each of them can make your visit better or worse, and trust me, you don't want worse. Tip four: respect your ER doctors because they're the only ones in the world who will treat you first and ask for payment later. And because of this, they get burned by one out of every three patients, and wind up losing $100,000 of income each year. Tip five: Be as honest as possible. If we ask how that hamster got stuck in your colon, it's not because we're judging your lifestyle. And finally, you should be aware that hospital stays are going to get worse every year than they were in the past."

"Why?"

"Because there are 1,100 fewer emergency rooms now than there were 20 years ago, and 33% more patients."

The conference room door opens.

It's Rose.

"Doctor, I hate to interrupt you, but the patient will be here in twelve minutes. We need to get scrubbed."

I say, "Ladies and gentlemen, this is my surgical assistant, Rose Stout. I'm afraid we have to conclude the discussion."

Everyone jumps to their feet again, only this time they're oohing and aahing over Rose's beauty, and wishing her well in the surgery. As they crowd around her, Rose frowns, and suddenly all the elderly are frozen in place.

"Shit!" she says.

"What's wrong?"

"Count them."

"What?"

"How many were here when you started?"

"Thirteen."

"And *now* how many?"

I count them. "Twelve."

"What does *that* tell you?"

"One's missing?"

"Exactly. And his name is Creed."

"What?"

"How could you not tell he was disguised?"

"I—are you *positive?*"

"It took me a moment to feel his presence. By then he was gone."

"What about Callie?"

"She wasn't here."

"You're certain?"

"I am. But that doesn't mean she's not in the hospital."

"Creed probably set this stupid meeting up so he could get his people into position."

"Gee, you think?" she says, sarcastically.

"The old people probably never even read an article about me."

"Gideon?"

"They probably just wanted a morning excursion and he told them to pretend I'm someone special."

"Don't pout."

"He probably offered them a pancake breakfast, or some such bullshit."

"Gideon!"

"What?"

"Snap out of it. Take a deep breath."

I do. Then say, "What now?"

"Stick to the plan. And if you really *do* have a Plan B, get it together quickly."

"Okay. Sorry. I'll meet you in the OR."

When she leaves, I place the calls required to put my backup plan in motion.

Chapter 29

I THOUGHT ABOUT my backup plan all night, and realized I was about to walk into another Creed trap. Not sure how, because I still don't have a handle on how many moves ahead Donovan Creed plans things. But it's certainly multiple, which tells me I have to think—again, pardon the pun—*outside the box.*

My original backup plan was logical, methodical, and therefore, utterly useless. I figured this out courtesy of the New England Patriots. I'm not a football guy, but while surfing TV channels last night I happened to catch a segment where two analysts were talking about how the Patriots blew away a superior opponent by doing something completely unexpected: they left their running and passing formations unchanged from the prior game. Everyone expected them to make changes, and the opposing team was shocked (and delighted) to see them line up in the most predictable manner possible. Except that when the game started, the Patriots passed out of their running formations and ran out of their passing formations! By halftime, the Patriots had a huge lead, so the opposing team made adjustments. Unfortunately for them, the Patriots also made adjustments, including abandoning their winning game plan in order to use formations they had never used before.

The result?

They beat the spread by more than 30 points.

I came away with two thoughts: first, I'm glad I'm not a football coach, and second, I realized my backup plan was a reaction to what I thought Creed might do if my first plan didn't work. In other words, I was falling into the same trap as the Patriots' opponent, and this realization helped me view things from a totally different perspective. I started by reminding myself that my Plan A relies 100% on my witchy friend, Rose. While that seems like a safe bet, it dawned on me that Rose has known Creed much longer than she's known me.

Could she possibly be working with him?

I know what you're thinking: she didn't call *me*, I called *her*.

But remember, Creed predicted with absolute certainty I'd steal Judson's car and race to his home, based on nothing more than past decisions I've made under similar opportunity-based circumstances. And let's be realistic: what are the chances Rose just *happened* to be at my house the same night Creed and Jackie Fish popped in?

Who knows? She's a fucking witch. Maybe she's been living in my penthouse for years, disguised as a chair. A better question is: with my back against the wall would it cross

Creed's mind that I'd call on Rose for help? Her being the one person on the planet more powerful than him?

Of course.

Not only that, he'd *expect* me to call her. And isn't that the type of plan Creed would embrace? To con *me* into securing Rose's help only to have her pull the rug out from under me?

It's exactly what he'd do.

Except, even Creed wouldn't go to this much trouble if he could count on Rose's help. If she were *really* his friend, why not ask her to kill Salib and his entire terror cell? I mean, how hard could *that* be for a witch?

The answer is I don't know. Might be very hard. Rose would be the first to tell you she has no super powers, just special abilities and heightened senses. Of course, that depends on how you define powers. Rose says we've all met people who can command our attention by simply entering a room. Is that a power or an ability? I say ability, and remind her she claims to be 300 years old, but only looks 30. She responds by saying Christy Brinkley's 61 and only looks 30. Is that a power? To be sure, there are lots of super-type powers Rose *doesn't* possess. For example she claims she can't freeze people if she can't see them, and if that's true she probably wouldn't be able to *kill* people she can't see. But maybe she's lying about that. Even so—and this is the biggest problem with using Rose—if she really *is* working for Creed, she'll be in the same room with me during the surgery. Which means—spoiler alert—she could simply freeze *me* during the surgery!

They could bring Baqir Salib into my operating room and Rose could freeze the nurses and me, and Baqir would die, and she herself could plant the bomb in his chest cavity. Again, I don't see this happening, but I'd be an idiot to rule it out. Bottom line: I realized my Plan B had to focus not on Creed, but on my own natural tendencies, and on Rose, the one I'm trusting to make things work.

And for this reason, my contingency plan needs to be foolproof.

And I think it is. Why? Because it relies 100% on the people who despise me! And that's why two of my phone calls just now were to Bruce Luce and Sylvia Beadle.

Bruce, you already know. I used my call to inform him that I spent twenty minutes this morning reviewing Baqir's chart and medical records the folks at Breighton Medical faxed to my office. I told him I don't want to use my regular staff for the upcoming surgery, but prefer a completely different group of nurses, as well as a neonatal nurse to stand by for possible after-care instructions. I told him I didn't care which nurses he chose to assist my surgery as long as they were qualified and apart from the original rotation. I also told him that the prenatal nurse he chooses will require full access to all areas of the hospital, and she'll have to follow my orders implicitly, which means Bruce will have to reassure her that no matter what I ask her to do, she won't get in trouble if Baqir dies. I told Bruce if he fails to provide exactly what I'm asking, I wouldn't be able to guarantee success.

Bruce said, "Let me make sure I get this right: if I give you what you want you'll *guarantee* the kid survives?"

"That's right."

Here's what you have to know about Bruce: while he wants me to fail, he can't deny my requests. Because if he refuses to provide what I ask, the child's death falls on him, not me. And if I guarantee success, and fail, he'll have another bargaining chip when it comes to replacing me. As I head to the dedicated OR that only I can use, I feel my phone buzzing in my pocket. I check caller ID and smile. It's Truth Luce. What are the chances she wants to set up another miracle massage?

One hundred percent?

I can't hardly wait.

As for her husband, whoever Bruce sends to assist my surgery will reveal all I need to know about him. Will he send me the most experienced nurses available? Or the least experienced? I've said some harsh things about him, but would he really risk the life of an innocent child to get me fired?

I think he might.

While losing one child isn't likely to get me fired, Bruce knows it would certainly be a major step in the right direction, so my guess is he'll give me the dregs, not the cream. But it doesn't matter which nurses he sends, since little Baqir's fate rests in the hands of two people: Rose and me. No one else's...provided the support nurses aren't planning to kill him.

Wait: *what?*

Oh yes! My Plan B factors in the likelihood that Creed may have threatened my regular staff of nurses. So if Bruce chooses a whole new staff for me at the last minute, I'm completely out of the equation. This is important because I'm sure Creed has not only studied *me*, but also our hospital, and almost certainly knows which nurses are on the current rotation, or which ones I might prefer to have in the OR with me. And all it takes is one bad nurse to kill a child during surgery. By singling out one or more of my regular nurses and kidnapping their kids or holding their families hostage, he could force them to botch the operation.

But he'd have no way of predicting which nurses Bruce Luce might pick for me at the last possible moment.

As for Bruce, my requests are music to his ears, since it reduces my chances for success. If Baqir dies, Bruce can use my requests to show the Board how incompetent I am.

To recap: if Rose is out to get me, I'm screwed. But even a cooperative Rose might not be enough if Creed has threatened the nurses. So the nurses—especially the neonatal nurse Bruce chooses—are vital to my Plan B. As for why I called Sylvia Beadle?

She's head of security.

I warned her of a possible terror threat and asked her to stand in front of my OR door to inspect every single item brought into the OR. I asked her to pay particular attention to Rose, knowing she'll want to bring her centuries old medical bag into the OR. I asked Sylvia to go through Rose's bag carefully and to run a metal-detector wand over her and each nurse before allowing them to enter my OR. I specifically asked her to be on the lookout for any type of weapon or small bomb that could be secreted into the room. I also asked her to have one of her associates film the entire procedure and have at least two other security personnel monitoring it, in the event anything suspicious happens.

"Like what?" she asked.

"Like maybe you find yourself unable to move a muscle, and the camera man stops filming. That will be security's cue to storm the OR and seal the building."

You'd think Sylvia would question this, but no, she's too excited. She loves being in charge, and embraces every opportunity to demonstrate her power.

Chapter 30

THE NURSES ENTER first, then Rose. Surprise number one is Bruce has selected a top-notch crew of nurses to assist my surgery. Perhaps it's because he doesn't want to have to explain to the Board why he chose the dregs instead of the most qualified. They're all staring bug-eyed at Rose's ancient medical bag. The reason this is a problem: the bag, and all the herbs, powders, and medicinals in it—have almost certainly contaminated our previously sterile environment. I tell the nurses: "Not a word about this to anyone."

Rose laughs and says, "Don't worry, Gideon. They won't remember anything that happens in this room. In fact, they've already forgotten."

"How's that possible?"

"Their minds are focused on granting our every request. Nothing else registers."

I give her a look. "You're saying they'll do whatever we ask?"

"Yes."

"Mind if I test that theory while we wait for the patient?"

"Please do."

I ask two of the nurses to kiss each other passionately. Without a moment's hesitation, these beastly women are going at it like their tonsils are on fire, and only their tongues can put out the flames. I tell them to stop and they do so immediately, and act as if nothing happened.

I look at Rose. "I could have really used you during the great blow job drought of the early 2000's."

"Too bad I didn't know." She cocks her head and says, "Here they come!"

Moments later I hear the critical care specialists outside the room with our tiny patient. I exit the room, check his ID bracelet, confirm it's Baqir Salib, and ask the critical care guys if they've been with him since the moment he left Breighton Medical.

They confirm they have.

I ask them to wait outside with Sylvia and guard the door until I come out. They look at me like I'm an idiot and one says, "Our job is delivery. Nothing else."

"Where's the mother?" I ask.

"In the waiting room."

As they walk away I tell Sylvia to take a picture of the kid's face. After she does I tell her: "Go to the waiting room, find Mrs. Salib, get her to confirm this is her son. If it is, knock three times on the door. If not, knock once."

She nods, and heads off to do what I asked.

I open the door and have the nurses get Baqir on the table and hook him up to all the equipment. While they do that, I read the chart carefully to make sure it's the one Breighton Medical faxed me this morning, and to see if they've added any notations since the last time I checked.

Everything's as it should be, and of course, that's what worries me.

Rose says, "What are you looking for?"

"Anything that tells me the chart might be phony."

"You're giving Creed a lot of credit."

"Wouldn't you?"

She nods. "I would indeed."

"If he got someone to slip us a phony chart, it would lead us in the wrong direction."

"True. So maybe you should ignore the chart altogether."

"That's risky," I say. "But I agree."

I go to the adjoining room and scrub in again, and when I return one of the nurses says, "We're ready, Doctor."

Rose looks at Baqir, then at me, and says, "You ready to save this little shit?"

"I am. Got any ideas?"

"Would you agree he's been poisoned?"

"Absolutely. But it would have to be a substance, or combination of substances that presents a delayed reaction. Any idea what Creed's poison of choice is these days?"

"Ricin, last I heard."

"Me too. But that's not what this is."

"Why not?"

"Too unreliable. Ricin takes up to three days to kill an adult. Baqir's tiny. He would've been dead within hours."

"Maybe Creed's contact administered a tiny dose."

"I don't think so."

"Time-release capsules?"

"Excellent thought, but no. Ricin doesn't mesh with the charts. They show initial vomiting and diarrhea. Ricin would be nonstop, with severe gastric pains."

"You said yourself the charts could be bogus."

"I did."

The head nurse says, "Doctor? The patient's going downhill fast."

Rose looks at me. "She's right. What do you want to do?"

"Notice anything missing?" I say.

"Like what?"

"The bomb."

"Creed didn't give it to you last night?"

"No."

"Then he's probably going to pay us a visit soon, or immediately following the operation." She pauses. "There's one other possibility."

"What's that?"

"He might have decided not to go through with it."

I laugh. "Does *that* sound like Creed?"

"It does not. But he knows I'm here to protect this child."

I give her a look. "You sure about that?"

"I already gave you my word."

"You did. Would you mind doing it again?"

"Normally, I would. But I can see you're stressed." She leans down, kisses Baqir's head. "I won't let anything happen to him, Gideon. You have my word. I'll protect him with my life."

"Thank you."

"Anything else?"

"Yeah. Why'd you bring that bag?"

"Same reason as always: it contains 300 years of alternative medicine, and it's helped us many times."

"Is there anything in there that strengthens the immune system?"

"Same thing I gave you a few months ago when that girl beat the shit out of you."

One of the nurses smirks, and I'd tell her off if I thought she was going to remember the comment after she leaves. But since she won't, I ask Rose: "Are you talking about your famous birch bark tea?"

She nods. "I can't brew it here, but I distilled a batch. I could administer the extract."

"Let's put some in a medicine dropper and see if we can get him to swallow it."

"Gideon?"

"Yeah?"

"Birch bark extract is an amazing remedy. But it takes days to work."

"Even for an infant?"

"Well, no, but we're still talking hours. And do I really have to remind you this little guy's on his last few minutes?"

"Give it to him anyway."

"Why?"

"Can't hurt."

"Okay. But...how long are you planning to stand there, doing nothing?"

"As long as it takes for him to die or get better."

She gives me a look. Says, "I don't understand."

"I'm not sure I do, either. But look at his abdomen."

"What about it?"

"It's untouched. No one's operated on him."

"Nor should they. Their job was to treat his symptoms and pass him off to you if he failed to respond."

"Exactly."

She takes a deep breath. "Your attitude is beginning to annoy me."

I say, "Creed expects me to operate."

"So do I."

"Right, and normally I would. I'd cut him open, search his organs for damage. But Creed knows that. More importantly, he requires an incision in Baqir's abdomen in order to implant the bomb."

"So?"

"I'm not going to give him one."

"You're going to let him die?"

"Yes."

"What am I missing?"

"Ever heard of Friar Lawrence from *Romeo and Juliet?*"

"What about him?"

"That's Creed. And this kid's Juliet."

She sighs. "Either Creed is totally in your head, or..."

"I'll explain while you give him the birch bark."

Chapter 31

"AFTER SAYING SHE'D rather die than live without Romeo, Juliet asked Friar Lawrence for advice. That gave him the idea to give her a potion to make her appear dead. He said after her family placed her in the tomb, Romeo could go there, wait for her to revive, then they'd go off together and live happily ever after. But Romeo didn't get the message."

We hear a triple knock at the door.

Rose gives me a questioning look.

I say, "This is definitely Baqir. His mother just identified him."

"Nice touch."

"Thanks."

"You think Creed gave Baqir a sleeping potion that mimics death?"

"I do."

"And how do you surmise Creed came upon such a potion?"

"Two possibilities: government scientists...or you."

"You think I'm helping him?"

"It crossed my mind."

"Is that why you had me searched?"

I nod.

She says, "I don't know of any potion that mimics death, and I doubt Creed does, either. If this is what you're counting on, I think you're making a huge mistake."

I set my jaw. "I guess we'll know soon enough."

"I gave you my word I'd protect this child. I'm not sure I can stand here idly and watch him die."

"I'm putting my trust in Creed. It would be just like him to give me a perfectly healthy baby boy who's certain to die the moment I start cutting on him."

"And if he dies on the table because we've done nothing to help him?"

"We'll do all we can to revive him."

"So your plan is to just stand here and see what happens?"

"That's the plan."

She takes a deep breath, lets it out slowly. "In that case shouldn't I freeze the nurses?"

"Please do."

As the minutes slowly tick by, Rose and I stand over Baqir, watch his vitals, and wait for his condition to improve or deteriorate. At one point I notice Rose holding a small container.

"What's that?"

She smiles. "Something from my bag. A sentimental favorite."

"Could it be useful in this situation?"

"I wouldn't think so."

"What is it?"

"Old silk from a Spider rain."

I cock my head. "Spider rain?"

She nods.

"I'm not familiar with the term."

"It's quite rare in nature. This sample is..." She pauses to do the math; then smiles. "150 years old."

"Are you saying it sometimes rains spiders?"

"Yes. But usually no more than a few hundred thousand at a time. This particular one had billions."

"That can't be possible."

"Believe it or don't, but I was there. It was a special event, created by a darling little girl as a gift to her father." She laughs. "You should have seen the look on his face when—"

Something catches her attention.

She leans over Baqir's body, presses her cheek to his head. "I'll be damned."

"What's wrong?"

"He's improving."

"Are you sure?"

"Positive. He's definitely on the mend."

"Nothing's showing up on the monitors."

"Give it a minute."

Sure enough, the monitors gradually start chirping their agreement. The grin on my face is infectious. Rose has one too, and gives me a warm hug. "Good for you, Gideon! I thought you'd lost your mind."

"I think I lost it years ago. But thanks."

"What now?"

"Can I trust you?"

She frowns. "I hope you're not planning to ask me a third time if I'm helping Creed kill this child."

"I just meant we haven't heard from Creed, haven't received the bomb, and that makes me nervous. He's probably waiting to see what happened. But when he finds out Baqir's alive, all bets are off."

"What are you saying?"

"I need to give Creed a bigger problem to worry about than this baby. I want you to stay here and stand guard while I meet the mom and tell her he survived."

"How will that help?"

"She'll tell her husband, he'll be emboldened to launch his attack, and Creed will do what he always does."

"What's that?"

"Find an alternate way to kill Salib and his crew."

She laughs, shakes her head. "I would have considered you too vain to give Creed that much credit."

I shrug, leave the room, and tell Sylvia not to let anyone through the door till I get back. Then I head to the waiting room to meet Baqir's mom.

Chapter 32

OF THE SIX women crying in the waiting room, Mrs. Salib's the loudest. She's sobbing inconsolably.

Time to put on my Superman Cape and be the hero I am. I approach her and say, "Mrs. Salib, I have good news. Your son's condition has improved."

She looks at me with grateful eyes, but can't stop sobbing.

"I'm optimistic."

She nods, but says nothing.

I go all in: "He's going to be fine."

Still nothing.

I look at the other women in the room, ask if anyone has any questions, but they ignore me and refuse to make eye contact. You might think it's a religious thing, but the truth is most women ignore me and refuse to make eye contact. Still, I'm a bit surprised no one seems particularly happy to hear the news. It's almost as if they *wanted* Baqir to die. That's not true, of course, because if they wanted him to die, they wouldn't have asked for me in the first place.

I chide myself for even saying that.

As I walk back to the room I can't help but wonder where Creed is. If he's ready to kill me, I'm ready to die. I'd just like a little notice first, since my nicotine tooth is in place, ready to be accessed.

Now, back in the OR, I'm pleased to find Baqir has made a dramatic improvement. Nevertheless, Rose and I monitor his condition for the next two hours. Not because we *need* to, but because I don't want to leave the OR before I *have* to. I figure two hours gives Mrs. Salib plenty of time to contact her husband.

I look at Rose. "It's halftime."

"Come again?"

"Time for us to do the unexpected."

I remove my cell phone from the pocket of my scrubs and...

I know what you're thinking: why would I have a cell phone in the OR? After all, cell phones interfere with the hospital's medical equipment, right?

Not true. I mean, I generally keep mine turned off if I'm within ten feet of an active EKG, but even *that's* probably overkill. So why do hospitals lie about the dangers of cell phones?

Because they can!

In other words, we know you'll believe us, because it sounds plausible, and we're counting on you to keep them turned off so you won't (a) record secret videos of gross negligence that could be used as evidence against us in court, (b) record our conversations, especially the ones where we explain your upcoming operation, since we're certainly not going to tell you all the details you'd want to hear and weigh before making a life and death decision. That could come back to bite us in court, as well. And (c) we also don't want you taking pictures of other patients without their consent, since they could sue us for allowing you to invade their privacy.

Since we can't think of a single way your phone use can help us, and twenty ways it could hurt us, we simply say that using your phone on our property could kill our patients. Admit it: that sort of talk scares the shit out of you.

So anyway, I turn on my cell phone and notice a second call from Truth Luce, a first from Gail Garner (whose husband, Harold, faked the back injury), but none from Creed.

I call the number I recently programmed, and Nurse Jennifer answers with, "I'm busy, Doctor."

"Glad to hear it. Nevertheless, I need you here in my OR." She says nothing, so I add: "On Millionaire's Row."

"I'm on duty," she says. "And even if I weren't, I don't have clearance."

"Are you in the middle of a life-and-death situation?"

"No."

"Good. Because I'm sending our head of security to fetch you."

"How will I know him?"

"It's a her. Sylvia Beadle."

"What should I bring?"

"Just your sweet self."

That gets her riled up. "Look, Gideon, if this is a ploy to—"

"Relax. This is completely legitimate. It's also an opportunity to get you into the big time."

She pauses a few seconds, then says, "I can be in the lobby in five minutes."

"Make it three."

Chapter 33

WHEN SYLVIA KNOCKS on the door, I open it and Nurse Jennifer enters.

"What's wrong with them?" she says, looking at the nurses.

Rose does nothing I can detect, but the nurses are suddenly checking the monitors and fussing over the baby as if they'd been lucid the entire time.

Jennifer does a double-take.

I tell the nurses to load up the cart for transporting the baby to the PACU.

The neonatal nurse says, "The baby seems fine, Doctor."

"Nevertheless, I want him to get the full treatment: oxygenation, ventilation, monitoring equipment. Then we'll transport him to the post anesthesia care unit."

The nurses look at each other. One says, "Did he receive anesthesia?"

I look at Rose, who does whatever it is she does, and within seconds the baby's in the cart, ready for transport. I tell Rose to freeze everyone, and make sure their memories are clear. Then I retrieve the doll I bought in the gift shop this morning and hid in my duffel bag, and have Rose remove Baqir from the cart and replace him with the doll. We cover the doll with a blanket and hat, and Rose wakes the nurses and gives them a subliminal message that the doll's an actual baby. She instructs them to transport the cart to the PACU while she follows closely behind. If Rose and the nurses make it to the PACU, she'll remain there to guard the doll. This way if Creed's people are nearby, they'll go after the doll, not Baqir. Meanwhile, Nurse Jennifer will stay in the Operating Room and monitor the baby until further notice. She'll have no memory of the other nurses, or the doll, or anything else that happened after she entered the OR.

I plan to leave at the same time as Rose and the nurses, and will instruct Sylvia to keep guarding the OR entrance and contact me if anyone attempts to enter. But instead of following them to the PACU I'll go to my office, where I expect Creed will be waiting to kill me.

Knowing this might be the last time I see her, I give Rose a hug and thank her for all she's done for me in the past, and for helping me save Baqir. Then I ask her to wait one minute before unfreezing Nurse Jennifer, and I take that minute to kiss Jennifer's lips and give her tits and ass a thorough fondling. When she comes to, she kicks and slaps the piss out of me and continues doing so until Rose finally makes her stop.

"Took you long enough," I say, wiping the blood from my nose and mouth.

"You deserved every bit of it," Rose says.

With Jennifer finally calm, I tell her to stay here and monitor Baqir's condition until further notice. Then the rest of us exit the room.

Chapter 34

AS I ENTER my office, I study my secretary's face and conclude if Creed's in my private office she—Lola—knows nothing about it.

"How was the surgery?" Lola asks.

"Successful."

"How stressful was it?"

Lola's not asking because she cares. She's asking because I've been known to go off the deep end following particularly stressful operations.

"I'm good," I say. "Any calls?"

"None that you'll want to fool with."

I nod, approach the door to my private office, take a deep breath, then say, "Lola, can you come in my office a minute?"

She frowns. "Why?"

"I...have this overwhelming..."

"Don't even think about it."

"What? Oh. Not that! I think someone might be in here. I'm concerned for my safety."

"But not mine?"

"It's hard to explain. I'm sure there's no one in my office or private bathrooms. But for some reason, I'm paranoid."

"Are you talking about the big, incredibly good-looking guy?"

I jump to the side of the door with my back against the wall, as if bullets might be flying through the door at any second. But Lola says, "He's not in there."

"You're certain?"

"Yeah. I wish he was, but he's not."

"But you *saw* him?"

She stares straight ahead. "I'm seeing him right now."

I dive face-first to the floor, try to scramble behind her desk. I look in the direction she'd been staring, but see nothing, even as she's saying, "What the *hell?*"

"Where is he?" I say.

"What?"

"The guy. You said you saw him just now. Where *is* he?"

She shakes her head. "You're never what I'd call sane, but these operations make you even worse. The man was here, he said a few words, then he left. I can still see him. In my *mind*, Gideon."

"He's not here?"

"No. But I wish he was." She sighs. "I'll never forget him."

I frown, get to my feet. "What did he say?"

"He said, 'Tell Dr. Box I'll be in touch.'"

I nod, enter my office, check behind the curtains, the couch, and the place under my desk where my chair goes. Then I check my private bathroom and shower.

Carefully.

I take a deep breath, let it out slowly.

Creed's not here.

My phone chirps, and I know with every fiber of my being it's Creed, texting me to meet him somewhere for the very last time.

But I'm wrong.

It's Truth Luce.

Normally I'd jump down her throat for serial texting me like this, but I'm so relieved it's not Creed I go straight to my desk and do what her message says: I call her.

As I indicated previously, Truth doesn't possess the type of looks that'll keep you hard all night, but she's pretty enough that you'd do her every time you had the opportunity. Her looks are venue-specific: if you need a woman to accompany you to the theater, symphony, opera, or elegant fund-raiser, Truth will be among the top 10% in terms of looks, style, class, and conversational ability. But if you're going to a night club, party, or statement event where only a trophy date will do, you'll want to go younger, hotter, and less uptight. My reason for bringing this up, I've been under a lot of stress in the last 28 hours, and having seen her naked last night has got me stirred enough that I'd be pleased to fuck her cross-eyed if she really wants another patch this badly.

Though now that I think about it, I can't imagine she needs additional pain medication this soon.

In fact, she couldn't.

More likely she's calling about the pain pills I promised to give her last night.

I press the call back key on my phone and Truth answers, saying, "How's your patient?"

"Really well. I think he's going to make a full recovery."

"You're truly amazing, Gideon."

"Thanks."

"I'm serious. They could never replace you."

"I agree. What's up? Are you calling about the pain pills? I was so pleased with your progress last night I forgot to give them to you."

"Strangely enough, I completely forgot about the pills. But now that you mention it, can I see you again in two days?"

"Absolutely." Thinking, *assuming I'm still alive.*

"Maybe I can get the pills while I'm there."

"That'll work."

"Thank you. The reason I called, you wanted me to keep you informed about what Bruce is up to."

"You've got something?"

"I do. And it's huge."

"Tell me."

"He hired your replacement."

"*What?*"

"I just found out he hired someone *weeks* ago. She's already started."

"*She?* That's impossible. If he hired *anyone* to replace me, I'd know. Especially a woman. The whole hospital would be talking about it."

"She's been working undercover."

I pause. "Are you hallucinating?"

"What do you mean?"

"The medication I gave you. I wouldn't expect hallucinations, but in higher doses it can lead to—"

"I'm not hallucinating, Gideon. Bruce hired someone weeks ago. Ostensibly she's replacing Dr. Casey, who was terminated last night, but she's really there to replace you, eventually. And she's been spying on you, helping Bruce gather information to use against you."

This can't possibly be true. But I decide to humor her by asking, "What's her name?"

"Jenny Cartwright."

"Never heard of her!"

"Maybe you should check her out."

"I will. Do you have any information on her? Like where she's from, where she trained, or how old she is, or—oh, shit!"

Chapter 35

"WHAT'S WRONG?" TRUTH asks.

"You're talking about Nurse Jennifer."

"No. Not a nurse, she's a doctor. Some sort of rising superstar in your field of expertise. But yes, Bruce started her off in the Emergency Room where she's been posing as a nurse. Until today, anyway."

"Let me get this straight: he planted her there just to spy on *me?*"

"Not just you, but yes, you were the primary target."

"What has she told him?"

"Nothing really bad, far as I can tell. I mean, nothing about pilfering drugs, at least. She said you tried to hit on her multiple times, and that you were constantly away from your post. She said you showed a shocking disregard toward the patients, and that you treated the nurses with a total lack of respect."

"She couldn't find it in her heart to say *anything* nice about my work?"

"She did say something about how you helped protect a couple of first year doctors who had compromised a patient. You removed a syringe from a patient's backbone or something?"

"I did. Is that everything?"

"Far as I know."

I breathe a sigh of relief. If Creed decides to let me live it'd be nice to continue practicing medicine, or at least have that option.

"Thanks, Truth. This is exactly the type of information I'm looking for. I think you and I are going to be friends for a long time."

"I hope so. But don't start celebrating too soon. Bruce says the Board loves her. Of course, that might change after this morning."

"Why's that?"

"You kicked her ass."

"What do you mean?"

"You didn't know it, but you and Dr. Cartwright were in a head-to-head competition this morning."

"Come again?"

"You both operated on critically ill patients at the same time. Yours made it, hers didn't."

"I don't understand."

"Two twin boys were admitted to the hospital this morning with identical symptoms. Yours lived, hers didn't. In fact, Dr. Cartwright's patient died within minutes. Apparently, the family's already claimed the body."

"*What?*"

"Game over, Gideon! Congratulations! You won! She's clearly not ready to take your place! But don't sell her short. I'm sure Bruce intends to keep her on staff, since she's already moved her stuff into Casey's old office."

I feel faint.

I end the call and run to the OR to find Jennifer holding the baby. One look at my face tells her I know she's not a nurse, so she says, "How did you know he didn't require surgery?"

I close the door behind me and say, "You switched the ID bracelets?"

She nods.

"How did Creed force you to do this?"

"He didn't. I volunteered."

That shocks me. "You're a doctor."

"If you're asking 'how can a doctor purposely kill a child?' I'll have to ask 'how can a doctor allow 10,000 citizens to die?'"

"Creed approached you? Out of the blue?"

She gives me a look that's almost pity. As if she can't believe I'm this naïve. Then says, "We've met before."

"What are you talking about?"

"I met you a couple of years ago."

I'm drawing a blank, so she says, "Donovan Creed's daughter? Kimberly? You came to Sensory Resources to try to save her life, but she was too far gone."

"You were there?"

"I'm the one who briefed you on her condition when you first arrived. That's why I didn't think this idea would work. I was positive you'd recognize me."

"I'm shocked I didn't."

"I have to give Creed the credit on this one. He said you wouldn't remember me because when we met you were madly in love with Trudy Lake, and terrified he was going to hold you responsible for his daughter's death. He said if I met you this week at Sensory, or if I showed up here as a doctor you might have made the connection. But if I entered your hospital as just another nurse..."

"So he put you in the ER instead of the hospital."

"Exactly."

Here we are, years later, and I'm *still* scared Creed's going to kill me. But I'm also mad as hell, and my mind's going 100 miles an hour, and yet I have to ask: "Are Creed and Bruce Luce working together somehow?"

"Not that I'm aware."

"Then how'd you know I'd wind up at the ER for five days?"

"We didn't. Donovan called Bruce and said he heard Bruce had been looking for a possible replacement for the famous Gideon Box. He said he had a world-class specialist who was off the grid, someone who could do the job."

I frown. "And Bruce hired you? Just like that?"

"Bruce interviewed me, of course, and checked out my resume. I think Creed's million-dollar donation helped get Bruce's attention, and he was anxious to move me right into the hospital. But Creed convinced him to plant me in the ER first, so I could get a feel for how things were being run.

Creed told him I could evaluate the ER doctors and nurses like no one else could, and that's when Bruce said he'd been thinking of making you work in the ER as punishment for something you'd done. Bruce asked me to keep an eye on you and report whatever I found. He was particularly concerned you might be stealing drugs." She locks her eyes on mine and says, "And you were."

Before I have a chance to protest, she says, "But I didn't tell him that."

"Why not?"

"Because I have no intention of working here, and to be completely honest, while I'm vastly superior to Dr. Casey, I couldn't possibly replace you in this role. And that's what I'll tell the Board on Monday when I submit my letter of resignation. And that should lock you into this position for a long time, assuming Donovan decides to spare your life."

"You think he will?"

"No. Can I ask *you* a question? No. Make that two questions."

I shrug.

"I already asked you the first one, but you failed to answer: how'd you know not to operate on this one?"

I think about saying it was a combination of intuition and knowing how Creed thinks, but before those words exit my mouth I realize how stupid they'd sound, so I tell her the truth: "Not knowing Salib had twins, I assumed this one was Baqir. Normally, I would have operated, but since there were no incision wounds on the body, I decided to screw Creed by giving him nothing to work with. No openings in which to implant the bomb."

"So—in order to beat Creed—you were willing to let this one die?"

"Not exactly. I believed Creed may have given him some sort of mystery drug that mimicked being poisoned, and presented symptoms of dying."

She studies me a moment. Then says, "Impressive."

"*Is* there such a drug?"

She says nothing.

"Please. I *have* to know."

"Sorry. I'm not authorized to discuss it."

"What's your second question?"

"What do you think Creed will do when he finds out you molested me in the OR?"

"Why should he care?"

"Because he's heroic when it comes to women...and because I'm his personal physician."

I shake my head. "Of course you are."

Again, I tell her the truth: "I assumed this would be my last day on earth and wanted to touch a beautiful woman one last time."

"Spoken like a true rapist," she says, and agrees I probably won't live to see the dawn.

I apologize for my impulsive behavior, and she more or less accepts it and confirms that the baby she's holding is Baqir's twin brother. "His name's Basim," she says, and doesn't deny Creed's contact forced both infants to ingest a dangerous substance.

She *does* admit Bruce Luce placed us in a head-to-head competition with the twins, and I suppose if I had failed and she succeeded, he might have been able to ease her into my job without skipping a beat. But of course, the contest was rigged, since Jennifer's job was to ensure Baqir's death.

Jennifer said Creed convinced Bruce not to tell me about the twins or the competition because I might try to sabotage her efforts. When the twins got to the hospital, she switched their ID bracelets to make sure she operated on Baqir, the firstborn. She killed him instantly, dismissed the nurses (she inherited the ones who'd been on my original rotation), sewed the bomb into Baqir's chest, and filled out the necessary paperwork to allow his body to be released to the family in time to pray over him for the proper length of time required by their religious beliefs. Creed facilitated this in advance by explaining to Bruce that Salib was a terror suspect, and the hospital could be in serious danger if they denied the request to remove the body.

Creed's behavior throughout this entire ordeal has been despicable. He's truly a monster, and I don't use that word lightly, since how else could you describe a man who worked this hard to kill a perfectly innocent child, and use his carcass to blow up his relatives and family members during a prayer ritual?

Having said that, I will admit he used his influence with Bruce to make sure Mrs. Salib remained at the hospital until her younger son, Basim, came out of surgery. In this manner he spared their lives and gave mother and son an opportunity to make a new beginning. According to Jennifer, he also provided a trust fund that will enable them to live comfortably for the rest of their lives.

Big deal.

It's nothing you and I wouldn't have done, aside from the money part, which I suppose makes Creed 1% less vile than he could be.

Speaking of Mrs. Salib, I reminded myself how I had Sylvia Beadle take the photo of the baby to her, and how she confirmed it was a true photo of her son. Of *course* it was, since Basim *was* her son. He just wasn't Baqir. I now realize that later on, when I told Mrs. Salib the good news that her son was going to be fine, the reason she hadn't appeared as grateful as I expected is because his twin brother—first-born Baqir—had died hours earlier, and the family was in a deep state of mourning.

All of which means I lost and Creed won.

Again.

Chapter 36

TWO DAYS LATER...

SINCE I'M STILL alive you might be able to figure out where I am, but in a million years you'd never guess what I'm doing. When Creed kept insisting he had future plans for me I assumed he was talking about how my elite surgical skills could benefit him somehow.

He wasn't.

But before I tell you that part, you'll want to know if Rose had prior knowledge I was operating on Baqir's twin brother.

The answer is, I have no idea.

She wouldn't say.

But she didn't seem shocked, or even surprised, so that might be a clue. Then again, Rose always plays things pretty close to the vest. She also has a dark sense of humor, evidenced by her behavior when I told her she no longer needed to pretend guarding the doll in post op. She made a big show of taking the doll to the center of the room, twisting its head off, and hurling it at one of the passing orderlies. He made a heroic effort to avoid being hit by what he thought was a human head, and everyone in the place screamed, leaving me to explain it was just a doll and it had been a stressful morning for all concerned.

Though I knew little Basim was on the mend before leaving him with Jennifer, I remained at the hospital another six hours to monitor his condition. When fully convinced he had made a complete recovery, I took the elevator to the doctor's parking garage, where one of Creed's henchmen was waiting for me with a gun.

And now I'm in a padded room in Creed's basement.

But again, you won't believe why he brought me here.

Go ahead, let your mind wander.

Doesn't matter, I could give you a hundred guesses and you'd still never get it.

My being alive tells you my suicide plan failed. It was rendered useless the moment I encountered the goon with the gun, because his gun turned out to be some sort of Taser, and he used it on me before I could get my hand to my tooth to scratch off the coating on the nicotine capsule. Then, after getting me into the back seat of his car, he gave me a shot that knocked me out. By the time I came to, I was in Creed's basement, and the capsule had been removed from my tooth.

So I'm stuck.

How do I know I'm in Creed's basement?

Trudy Lake told me. Trudy's my former girlfriend, currently going by the name Trudy Creed.

"He *adopted* you?" I asked.

"Married me," she said.

She had a baby with her that she claimed was hers, but I know better, since Rose and I delivered this very baby more than a year ago. Her name is Hawley, and Trudy's not the only one who claims parentage, since Rose considers Hawley to be *her* daughter.

"I bought her fair and square," Rose told me back then, and this was confirmed by the baby's actual mother, a New York City call girl named Miranda Rodriguez. Then yesterday I learned for the first time that Hawley's biological father is...

Donovan Creed.

My connection to these women runs deep, and might be a contributing factor in Creed's decision to imprison me. Miranda? I used to pay her for sex, unaware she was Creed's girlfriend, and favorite hooker at the time.

Trudy? I used to pay her $20,000 a month to live with me for the purpose of having regular sex. We didn't go "all the way," but we certainly went far enough sexually to more than annoy Creed.

And Rose claims to be Creed's direct ancestor, through some pirate named Jack Hawley, who plied his trade in the waters around St. Augustine, Florida, some 300 years ago.

To put it another way, I've enjoyed oral sex with Creed's current wife, fucked his former girlfriend, the mother of his child, and fucked his grandmother, twelve times removed.

Boxed In!

Can you blame him for wanting to punish me?

Chapter 37

SO HERE I am, secured to a padded wall in a room in Creed's basement, and...

I'm not alone.

I'm with...are you ready for this?

I'm with Creed's baby.

That's right, it's just the two of us, me and Baby Hawley, here in the padded room.

This is the "higher purpose" Creed had for me: to sit on the floor of a room for hours on end, while his daughter sits across the room and stares at me.

To be precise, she's not just staring. She's sifting through my brain.

It's not excruciatingly painful, nor is it pleasant. It feels a lot like when you've got a splinter, and someone's fussing over with it with a needle, trying to remove it. Except that this is my brain, and she's picking at thousands of little splinters, one after the other.

What's she searching for, data? Memories? Feelings? Experiences?

Beats me.

The way Trudy explained it, she's *copying* data. Apparently this child comes from a long line of healers and medical practitioners, and Trudy and Creed want to feed her thirst for knowledge.

But could she also be *removing* specific memories?

It's certainly possible, but...how would I know? I mean, if I suddenly couldn't remember my *name* it would be obvious she was removing information, because everyone knows their name, address, phone number, and other specific information. But if she happens to remove my understanding of an obscure medical procedure, or some detailed article I've read in the past, I'd have no way of knowing. I'd assume these were things I never knew in the first place.

She certainly hasn't removed my ability to understand time, because this process continues day after day, for hours at a time. Through it all, Baby Hawley's expression rarely changes. She just lays in her carrier and stares at me with those giant jade-green eyes and I feel the itchy, tingly, probing sensation that tells me someone's sharing my brain.

Sometimes I stare at her and think the words *Fuck You!* as hard as I can, and sometimes I shout at her, curse and threaten her, hoping she'll fail to gain access to whatever it is she seeks, but it never seems to work.

I haven't seen Creed a single time since I arrived. Every day it's just Trudy and the baby, and Trudy hasn't spoken since the second visit. She carries the baby in, leaves, then comes back hours later, gets the baby, leaves. Apart from that the only human interaction I have is with a man I assume is Creed's major domo, who removes me from the room twice a day for an hour, during which time I'm taken to a larger room, a gym, where I'm allowed to shower, exercise, use the bathroom, and eat a meal. Once a day he shaves me, and sometimes a nurse shows up to draw blood, or give me a shot or some pills, and then it's back to the prison room.

Lately Baby Hawley hasn't showed up, and I've been wondering if maybe she finished extracting all the information she wanted. I used to hate being in the room with her, watching her stare at me with those giant eyes, but now I miss her visits like crazy.

That major domo guy stopped showing up a while back, and now it's a different guy, or another different guy. Sometimes I lose track of how many different people Creed has sent to look in on me from one day to the next, but no matter who shows up, I always try to engage him or her in conversation. But they never respond. They're like robots, programmed to do their job, and nothing more.

I should probably mention the only time I've actually been secured to the wall was when Baby Hawley was alone in the room with me. The rest of the time I've been free to sit in the chair or sleep on the bed unrestrained.

I should also point out there are no mirrors, windows, or sharp objects of any kind, and it goes without saying I'd kill myself in the space of a minute if only I could, because the boredom of being confined like this, with no outside influences whatsoever, is practically unbearable. I know Creed threatened to punish me slowly and painfully, and

I'm sure he fully intends to keep that promise. The strange thing is, even knowing how horrific it'll be, I can't wait for him to start.

If Baby Hawley has finally finished with me Creed has no reason to keep me alive, so every time the door opens I expect it to be him, coming to torture me. Will he skin me alive? Feed me to rats? Shatter a different bone in my body each day till they'll all broken? Water board me to within an inch of my life over and over?

Who cares?

Anything would be better than this.

Chapter 38

TODAY SOMETHING NEW happens. I wake up feeling euphoric. Suddenly the door opens, and I'm surprised to see a beautiful little girl with the kindliest face. She focuses her jade-green eyes on me, takes a deep breath, and suddenly there's a bright aura around her. The light appears to be coming from her, and just being in her presence makes me feel years younger. As the light increases, it becomes so bright I can barely make out her features. When she speaks I can't believe my ears, because, incredibly, she asks, "Would you like to leave today?"

I stare at her blankly. Could I have heard her correctly?

She repeats, "Would you like to leave?"

I nod.

"Very well, I'll make the arrangements."

I can't believe what I'm hearing. Not just because of the message, but because of her vocabulary. I mean, the girl can't be more than five years old.

"Who are you?" I ask.

"Hawley Creed."

I do a double-take. "That's not possible!"

"Why not?"

"I saw you last week!"

"You think?"

"What are you, five?"

"I suppose I might appear that age to you."

I stare at her, and frown. "Is this some sort of sick joke? Creed's toying with me, isn't he!"

"If you're referring to my father, he passed away many years ago."

"Donovan *Creed?*"

She nods.

"I saw him days before arriving here."

"Yes."

"Then how could he have possibly been dead for years?"

She says, "How long do you think you've been here?"

I shrug. "I don't know. Two months?"

She laughs. "Sixty years."

"Excuse me?"

"My father wanted to punish you by making you sit here till you turned 100. But you taught me so much during those first sessions I decided to take pity on you and made the time pass in a much gentler manner. Though you've been here 60 years, you've barely aged. But my father promised you torture, and despite the fact I abhor violence, I'm honor bound to fulfil his promises. Therefore, torture is exactly what you'll get."

Nothing she says makes the least bit of sense, so I say nothing, and let her continue: "When you leave this room you'll immediately start aging. All the pains and illnesses you would have experienced over the past 60 years will hit you all at once. It will be...excruciating. By the time you get to our crematorium you'll be happy to be burned alive. And you will be. Unfortunately, it will take place over the lowest of flames. Then your ashes will be collected and sealed in an indestructible box—get it? A box? And this box will make a small screaming sound when shaken that's irresistible to primates. The reason this is important is because the box will be placed in chimpanzee playgrounds and habitats in order that your ashes will never be allowed to rest. These were my father's wishes with regard to your demise. Any questions?"

"Yes. If what you say is true, how can you possibly be five years old?"

"Remember your friend, Rose Stout? She and I age approximately one year for every fifteen years the general population ages." She pauses. "Is there anything else you'd like to ask?"

"Yes. You admitted taking pity on me once before. Is it outside the realm of possibility to ask you to spare me the pain of instantly aging 60 years? I can't imagine having my bones and organs deteriorate that much at the same time. If you abhor violence as you claimed, then surely you abhor needless suffering."

"Needless?"

"Your father's dead. You've already honored his wishes by keeping me here all these years, which means I've missed a lifetime of experiences I'll never get back. If you're being honest about how long I've been here, I'm a hundred years old. Surely you can allow me to live the rest of my days as a free man. Can't you?"

"Not a chance. My father gave his life to protect our nation, and saved millions of lives in the process. But it took a horrible toll on him. Killing that child 60 years ago was one of the worst decisions he ever had to make. And you made it much harder on him than it had to be. But more importantly, you owed him a favor and failed to fulfil it even after he gave you numerous and adequate warnings there would be consequences for your actions. Yes, I made your life a million times easier than it would have been had I not intervened, and my father never knew. But I owe it to him to make sure you suffer."

"Fine, whatever. I mean, how bad can it be?"

"Well...really bad. You'll experience a broken leg, broken ankle, broken ribs, the pain of several operations, a particularly nasty cut and ensuing infection, and a nasty bout of shingles." She pauses, then adds: "Two heart attacks, countless bouts of diarrhea and vomiting, sore throats, strep throats, colds, flu, pneumonia, back aches, tooth extractions, root canals, rheumatoid arthritis, and colon cancer. I'm sure I've left some out, but you get the point. All these pains will hit you at the same time. Under normal circumstances, you'd die. But I can't allow that on my watch."

"Thanks for elaborating. How long will your watch last?"

"Sixty years."

"Excuse me, did you say *sixty?*"

She nods.

"*Years?*"

She nods again.

"Shit."

"Exactly."

"One last request?"

"Go ahead."

"Can I at least go outside for a few minutes before it starts?"

"Why?"

"I'd give anything to see the sky one last time."

"Sorry, that's not part of the deal. Anything else?"

"Yes. Do you have any idea how stupid you look?"

She cocks her head. "What do you mean?"

"You're five years old, talking like a grown up. It's incongruous."

"Why?"

"You haven't even had your period."

"Thank you, Dr. Box."

"For what?"

"I expect I'll ponder that remark many times over the next sixty years. Any last words?"

"Yeah. Did you know I fucked your mother?"

"Yes. I had full access to your mind for weeks, remember?"

"She was a hooker. A prostitute. A *whore!*"

"So were you. Anything else? Be sure to get it all out before the screaming starts."

"I do have one last observation."

"Go ahead."

"You realize what this means, don't you?"

"What's that?"

"I finally won."

"Won what?"

"I'm still here and your father isn't."

"So?"

"It means I beat him. I won."

She laughs. "Glad you think so. Ready?"

I take a deep breath. Then say, "Do your worst."

THE END

...Well, except for this:

Epilogue

AFTER BOX SAID "Do your worst," she waited a full minute, then turned and exited the room. The guard locked the door behind her, escorted her up the stairs, and remained by her side until she entered the den.

Now she looks at the man and woman sitting on the couch and says, "Was that good, Mr. Creed?"

"You were perfect!"

"All I did was stand there and wait for the voice to talk and then to stop talking."

"That's all you had to do. But you did it well."

"The light sort of hurt my eyes."

"Well, I'm sorry about that, but you were wonderful. It was an excellent scene."

The girl's mother says, "When do you think the movie will be released?"

"I have no idea. Sometimes these movies get made, sometimes they don't. But the money spends just as well either way."

She smiles. "I can't believe such a small scene pays so much! Especially one without dialogue. Who supplied the voice?"

"Believe it or not, a twenty-five-year-old."

The woman shakes her head. "That's amazing. She sounded exactly like a little girl." She frowns. "Other than the subject matter, which was decidedly mature."

Creed says, "Like your daughter, she's a gifted actress." He pauses, then says, "I want to remind you about the contract you and your husband signed that stipulates you're not allowed to speak about this scene or movie to anyone until you receive written permission. Otherwise, your daughter will never work in Hollywood again, and you'll be responsible for returning the entire sum you've been paid. You understand this?"

"Yes, of course."

They talk a few more minutes, then Creed summons Anson, his majordomo, to drive them back to the airport. Moments later, Callie Carpenter enters the room.

Creed says, "Congratulations! You nailed it!"

She laughs, then uses her little girl's voice to say, "Thanks, Daddy. Want to powder my little butt?"

Creed smiles, shakes his head. "You're too much."

Callie says, "All jokes aside, I would've killed them."

"The kid and her mom? Why?"

"I don't trust them."

"You don't trust anyone."

"Neither should you. Especially that kid."

"Why?"

"She's creepy."

"She's five."

"Maybe so, but she saw Box's face. And his disappearance has been all over the news."

"Yes it has, but not lately. And anyway, we disguised his face with the beard and markers. She'll never be able to identify him as Box." He goes silent a moment; then says, "So why don't you trust the mom?"

"Mainly because she's a mom. I guarantee you, next time she's around her friends she's going to brag on her kid."

"We'll keep an eye on her."

"If she screws up, can I kill her?"

"Sure."

"Thanks. Did you happen to catch my mistake?"

"Yeah. Box said you hadn't got your period yet and you said 'Thank you, Dr. Box.' We didn't want the girl and her mom to hear his name, but it's not a problem. I told them Box is the nickname we gave the villain because Dr. Box went missing and this guy's character went missing. I said it was like an inside joke for the medical profession."

"You don't think she'll wonder about it as time goes on?"

He shrugs. "Like I said, we'll keep an eye on her."

"I think that's wise. As for Hawley..."

"Yeah?"

"No offense, but that's one freaky daughter you've got."

"That's quite a compliment, coming from you."

"Thanks again. I'm still curious as to how you think she's supposed to age. You originally told me she'll age normally, but we told Box she'll look 5 when she's 60."

"The answer is we don't know. Rose says she'll probably age normally till she's around ten, at which time she'll only age a year for every fifteen years the rest of us age."

"How does Rose know?"

"According to Rose, that's how she aged. But Hawley's ancestor, Scarlett Rose, had similar powers and aged normally her entire life. So there's no way to know for sure till it starts happening."

"Personally I don't believe any of it."

"That's your prerogative."

"Obviously. But I worry about you. I can't imagine you truly believe she accessed Box's brain."

"Let's just say I'm keeping an open mind about it."

"But you think it's possible."

"I'm entertaining that thought, yes."

"So you're claiming your infant daughter knows as much about surgical procedures as Gideon Box."

"*Rose* is claiming it, not me. But that doesn't make Hawley a surgeon. In other words, she has all the knowledge she needs, but no skills."

"So she's like what, a literary critic?"

"Exactly."

"Here's the part I'm trying to figure out: whose side is Rose on? Yours or Box's?"

"Neither. She only wants what's best for the child."

"And who gets to decide that?"

"She thinks she does."

"Uh huh. Well, since Rose clearly has powers none of us fully understand, that would scare the shit out of me."

"I agree. Welcome to my world."

Callie laughs, stops; then laughs again and says, "Box has to be a moron to think he's been held prisoner for 60 years."

"Two months of drug cocktails will throw anyone off their game. Not to mention the daily hypnosis sessions. Did you notice him looking at his hands and arms when you said he was a hundred years old? In his mind he could *see* the wrinkles."

"Does Trudy know he's still here?"

"Of course not."

She frowns. "I almost hate to say it."

"Go ahead."

"You need a woman who can handle these sorts of things."

"Trudy handles things just fine."

"Really? Then maybe we should tell her what's going to happen to her boyfriend."

"Ex-boyfriend."

"When will she be back from her shopping spree?"

"Doesn't matter: we're not telling her."

Callie arches a brow. "What if she finds out on her own somehow?"

"Don't even think about it."

"You're no fun."

"I think you'll change your mind about that in five minutes."

Callie's face lights up. "Does that mean we're going to do this *together?* Right *now,* while he's unconscious?"

"That's what it means."

She grins and gets to her feet. "I love it! We'll bust him up now, and when he wakes up it'll seem like all the aches and pains are coming at once, just like we promised. What's first on the menu for Dr. Box?"

"What's the first thing you promised him? Broken leg, broken ankle, broken ribs?"

"Uh huh."

"We can start with that."

"Can I break his ribs?"

"I don't see why not. You practiced that little girl voice for months. You've earned the right."

"I don't mean to sound greedy, but we promised tooth extractions."

"Did we?"

"Uh huh. How many can I pull?"

"What number suits you?"

"All of them."

He laughs. "Make it two. I plan to send him back to work, after all."

"You do?"

"Of course. He's still the world's greatest surgeon. Still the only one who can save those hopeless-case infants."

"But you brought him here as a punishment, right?"

"My main reason was to let Hawley access his brain. I had originally planned to wait a few years, but after observing Box's crazy lifestyle and erratic behavior, I was concerned he might not live long enough for her to do a full-scale probe."

"Assuming she did."

"Right. It's possible Rose has been lying about Hawley's abilities, or is simply wrong. But as for keeping Box prisoner, let's not forget he did everything I expected him to do. It would be unfair of me to be too upset with him."

"He refused your favor!"

"Yes, but I wanted him to."

"Why?"

"I had to ensure one of the twins lived. Otherwise, Salib would have thought something was up."

She sets her jaw. "The fact remains you asked him to perform a favor and he refused."

"Yes. And that's why we've kept him isolated from the world for two months, and why we're going to punish him now."

"Doesn't seem like enough."

"Don't fret. He's not completely off the hook."

"What do you mean?"

"My doctors will treat his injuries, but he's going to suffer through his recovery with no pain medication. Then, when it's time to clue him in on what we've done, I'll give him a choice: he can stay in my basement and receive the full 60 years of torture we promised, or he can go back to his former life."

"What's the catch?"

"If he chooses his former life, he'll owe me an Ultimate Favor."

She laughs. "Remind me to stay on your good side."

"Don't I always?"

Creed stands, walks to his desk; takes a key from his pocket, unlocks a drawer, removes a small leather case.

"What's that?"

"Two hypodermic needles, two vials."

"Containing?"

"A particularly nasty flu virus, and a toxin that mimics the symptoms of Shingles, only worse." He looks at her. "Ready?"

She smiles. "I was *born* ready."

THE END

Personal Message from John Locke:

I love writing books! But what I love even more is hearing from readers. If you enjoyed this or any of my other books it would mean the world to me if you'd click the link below so you can be on my notification list. That way you can receive updates, contests, prizes, and savings of up to 67% on eBooks immediately after publication!

Just access this link: http://www.DonovanCreed.com, and I'll personally thank you for trying my books.

Also, if you get a chance, I hope you'll check out Dani's website:

http://www.DaniRipper.wordpress.com

John Locke

New York Times Best Selling Author

8th Member of the Kindle Million Sales Club

(Members include James Patterson, George R.R. Martin, and Lee Child)

John Locke had 4 of the top 10 eBooks on Amazon/Kindle at the same time, including #1 and #2!

...Had 6 of the top 20 books <u>at the same time</u>!

...Had 8 books in the top 43 <u>at the same time</u>!

...Has written 30 books in five years in <u>six separate genres</u>, <u>All best-sellers</u>!

...Has been published throughout the world in numerous languages by the world's most prestigious publishing houses!

...Winner, Second Act Magazine's Story of the Year!

...Named by Time Magazine as one of the "Stars of the DIY-Publishing Era"

Wall Street Journal: "John Locke (is) transforming the 'book' business"

John Locke

New York Times Best Selling Author
#1 Best Selling Author on Amazon Kindle

Donovan Creed Series:

Lethal People
Lethal Experiment
Saving Rachel
Now & Then
Wish List
A Girl Like You
Vegas Moon
The Love You Crave
Maybe
Callie's Last Dance
Because We Can!
This Means War!
Boxed In!

Emmett Love Series:

Follow the Stone
Don't Poke the Bear
Emmett & Gentry
Goodbye, Enorma
Rag Soup

Dani Ripper Series:

Call Me!
Promise You Won't Tell?
Teacher, Teacher
Don't Tell Presley!
Abbey Rayne

Dr. Gideon Box Series:

Bad Doctor
Box
Outside the Box
Boxed In!

Other:

Kill Jill
Casting Call

Kindle Worlds:

A Kiss for Luck (Kindle Only)

Non-Fiction:

How I sold 1 Million eBooks in 5 Months!

www.ingramcontent.com/pod-product-compliance
Lightning Source LLC
Chambersburg PA
CBHW071143170626
46809CB00002B/748